SF 4

More Armada 'Spinechillers'

Armada Sci-Fi 1, 2 and 3
Edited by Richard Davis

Armada Ghost Books Nos. 1 – 9
Edited by Christine Bernard and Mary Danby

1st Armada Book of True Ghost Stories
A Shiver of Spooks
Edited by Christine Bernard

1st, 2nd and 3rd Armada Monster Books
Edited by R. Chetwynd-Hayes

SF 4

Science Fiction Stories

Edited by Richard Davis

Illustrated by Jim Cawthorn

Armada

SF 4 was first published in
the U.K. in Armada in 1977 by
Fontana Paperbacks,
14 St. James's Place, London SW1A 1PF

Printed in Great Britain by
Love & Malcomson Ltd., Brighton Road,
Redhill, Surrey.

CONTENTS

ACKNOWLEDGEMENTS

The editor gratefully acknowledges permission to reprint material from the following:

Harvey Unna and Stephen Durbridge Ltd., for DAGGER IN THE DEPTHS and MONSTER IN THE WOOD © Rosemary Timperley 1977

Michael Bakewell and Associates Ltd., for SPACE PIRATE © Martin Martinsen 1977, TOYS OF THE EARTH © Pamela Cleaver 1977, A CROCODILE EGG © John Halkin 1977 and THE INVASION OF THE TEDDY BEARS © Glenn Chandler 1977

Mrs. Rosemary Bromley, Juvenilia Literary Agency for FROM THE DEEPS © Wendy Eyton 1977

David Campton for YOU BE ME © David Campton 1977

Catherine Gleason for PROJECT 9 © Catherine Gleason 1977

Roger Malisson for THE INVASION and SOMETHING QUEER ON THE MOOR © Roger Malisson 1977

INTRODUCTION

In this fourth collection of Science Fiction stories written specially for you, I can promise you another mixture of strange worlds and even stranger beings.

We have tales which are set on Earth and tales which are set way out in Space – like *Space Pirate*, by Martin Martinsen, a 'whodunit' set on a remote planet. See if you can guess who the mysterious space pirate is before the author tells you. On the other hand, *Dagger in the Depths*, by Rosemary Timperley, is about Inner, rather than Outer Space. The strange world under the sea still holds many secrets for us. It certainly amazes the crew of a deep-sea submarine who are rescued from trouble by a very strange monster indeed. *Or are they?*

The monster in *Monster in the Wood* is a very different creature. In fact he's a hapless professor. Exactly how he had the misfortune to become one, we'll leave you to find out for yourselves. It all goes to show that you can't be too careful when messing about with scientific experiments.

Another rather crucial mistake occurs in David Campton's *You Be Me;* and this time it's made by a Time Traveller. Imagine being visited by your great-great-great-grandson, and then, when it's time for the visit to end, finding yourself being whisked away into the future because everyone thinks he's you! There's a link between this story and Pamela Cleaver's *The Toys of Earth*. I think you'll be very surprised to find out this particular space traveller's secret.

When you read *Invasion of the Teddy Bears*, by Glenn Chandler, take a second look at your old teddy. Is he *really* as harmless as he seems? And the same warning applies to Mr. Prendergast, in Catherine Gleason's *Project 9*. Only Mike can see that his schoolmaster isn't his schoolmaster at all. *But who is he?*

Eggs are not normally frightening objects. But there's something very spinechilling indeed about John Hálkin's *A Crocodile Egg* . . . And Helen, in *From the Deeps*, by Wendy Eyton, discovers that the unusual-looking shell she picks up on the beach also holds a terrifying secret, for it belongs to a very different world from ours.

There are two stories by Roger Malisson and bringing up the rear is one which we hope will end the book for you on a chuckle – proving that to be good, science fiction needn't necessarily be serious *all* the time.

I hope that you enjoy *SF 4* and that maybe – just, maybe – if ever you find yourself as an astronaut exploring new planets, you might see something that makes you say to yourself: "I know about this. I first read it in Armada!"

May, 1977   *Richard Davis*

THE INVASION OF THE TEDDY BEARS

by GLENN CHANDLER

The Great Teddy Bear Invasion never was supposed to be funny. It was intended to be taken with deadly seriousness, for the planet Earth was to find itself the target of a confident and highly mechanised battle fleet. Here's what happened.

The invasion force crept down at 6.30 on a summer Saturday morning, by a forest just outside the peaceful English village of Nether Hopling. Only one person saw it arrive – the village milkman, beginning his round – and he thought it was a flock of ducks. English villages were not generally chosen as landing sites for interplanetary invasion fleets, and, besides, he didn't believe in flying saucers.

The three craft hovered over the broken roof of the forest, then dropped silently into its leafy glades, observed by no eyes other than those of the birds and animals who lived there. The forest hushed; half a mile away the village was waking to the sound of milk bottles clinking on stone steps. The saucers waited. Their occupants planned. Then, at precisely 7.32 a.m., the hatches opened, and the planet Earth took its first look at a Megatoid.

The Megatoids were (and are) the most ruthless creatures in the universe. They were as near to being robots as any flesh and blood creature could be. They were also the most advanced species ever to have evolved on any planet; they were thoroughly hostile, devoid of emotion, cruel, precise, disciplined, trained in all branches of warfare, murderous, merciless and military. The trouble was, and the poor things weren't to know it, they looked like teddy bears. Standing just twelve inches off the ground, with their furry, dumpy legs, upraised arms, soft button noses and little blue jackets, they belonged in a toyshop window, not in an alien spacecraft. But, well, there was no way of telling a Megatoid this. You couldn't tell a Megatoid anything. He (sorry, it) would disintegrate you before you could say Pooh.

9

At 8.26 a.m. on this summer morning, the Megatoid army assembled. There were eighty of them, and they marshalled themselves into four companies of twenty; one would march west, one east, one north and one south. That was the Megatoid way of doing things. No messing. Just march off in a straight line and invade everything in sight. Anyone who crossed their path was deemed a prisoner. So it was, then, that a command of twenty ferocious but rather fluffy bears lined up to march west on Nether Hopling.

"MEGATOIDS – PROCEED – TO – SITE – OF – HABITATION!" ordered Number One in a cold, metallic voice, and the company began to goose-step through the forest, their dumpy legs pad-pad-padding on the bracken floor, their arms swinging, their noses held regimentally aloof. Birds popped out of nests to watch, animals crept out of their holes, and the whole forest became alive like one of those Happy Moments in a Disney cartoon when everything in the forest comes out and sings.

The Megatoids did not appreciate it.

"DISINTEGRATE – ALL – TWITTERING – LIFE – FORMS!" cried Number Two, and the Megatoids raised their weapons and pointed them into the treetops. Nothing happened. Triggers were pulled, but the birds and animals of the forest just sat and waited.

"DISINTEGRATION – SYSTEMS – INEFFECTIVE – IN – EARTH – ATMOSPHERE –" observed Number Three, noticing that his gun had failed to go off.

"DISINTEGRATION – SYSTEMS – UNNECESSARY –" followed Number One. "MEGATOIDS – ARE – THE – MOST – SUPREME – BEINGS – IN – THE – UNIVERSE. WE – SHALL – STRIKE – TERROR – INTO – THE – EARTHLINGS. THEY – WILL – SURRENDER TO – OUR – AUTHORITY. NOTHING – MAY – STAND – UP – TO – THE – MIGHT – OF – THE – MEGATOIDS. NOTHING!"

There was a shrill but rousing chorus of "NOTHING!" as they marched on through the forest, slashing out their defiance on the tall ferns and trampling their might upon the bluebells and buttercups. Eventually, they arrived at the edge, where a country road ran into the High Street of Nether Hopling. A van rose over the crest of a hill, and dipped, travelling fast towards them.

"EARTH – CRAFT – APPROACHING – " warned

Number One. "ASSUME – DEFENSIVE – POSITION!"

"WE – OBEY!"

They set themselves up in a line across the road, and stood with their dumpy legs apart and their disintegration guns aimed at the approaching van.

John Higgins and his son Mark could hardly believe their eyes at first. Strange things happened in the country – sheep and cows blocked the road – but teddy bears? Mr. Higgins slowed and stopped. He and Mark got out of the van and looked closely. Mr. Higgins scratched his head in bewilderment.

"They *are* teddy bears," said Mark. "Somebody's put a line of teddy bears across the road."

"SILENCE!" came a command from Number One, who stepped forward. "YOU – ARE – OUR – PRISON-ERS. YOU – WILL – OBEY!"

"Listen, it speaks," said Mr. Higgins, crouching and looking the little bear in the eyes. They were like glassy beads, the sun glinting on them.

"I – SAID – SILENCE. REPEAT. YOU – ARE – OUR – PRISONERS. YOU – WILL – OBEY!"

"Maybe they fell off the back of a lorry, Dad," suggested Mark. "You could almost swear they were alive. Where do you wind them up?"

Mr. Higgins picked up the Megatoid, turned it upside down and searched for a key.

"PUT – ME – DOWN! PUT – ME – DOWN!" it cried out, and began to struggle violently for all its size. Mr. Higgins was so startled that he dropped it, and it landed on its head.

"It even feels alive," he told his son. "They must be radio-controlled. It must be a publicity stunt. Some new toy."

"Out here, Dad?"

"Maybe they went astray."

The Megatoid stood upright again; it was incapable of humiliation, but it had certainly felt a bang on the head.

"SURROUND – THE – PRISONERS!" it dictated, and the Megatoids obeyed. John Higgins and his son Mark found themselves encircled by the little bears. Mark was utterly delighted. He was too old for teddy bears, but walking-talking ones were exciting toys for any generation. A gleam in his father's eyes demonstrated that too, as he beheld the score of furry, upturned faces.

11

"WHY – DO – THE – EARTHLINGS – SMILE?" asked Number Three.

"PERHAPS – THEY – ARE – BRAINLESS – " Number Two put forward.

"THEY – HAVE – NOT – SHOWN – INITIAL – SIGNS – OF – FEAR – " observed Number One. "PROCEED – TO – TEST – REACTIONS – IMMEDIATELY!"

The Megatoids growled. It was most unfortunate. Any credibility they had hoped to recover was swept away in the effort.

"Listen to them all growling, Dad," said Mark, lifting one up for himself, and examining it.

"DISINTEGRATE – DISINTEGRATE – DISINTEGRATE!" shouted the Megatoid as it was turned this way and that, and squeezed for the feel of a motor under its fur.

"YOU – WILL – TRANSPORT – US – IN – YOUR – CRAFT – TO – THE – NEAREST – SITE – OF – HABITATION!" commanded Number Four. Mark put the Megatoid down, and the company of twenty filed into the rear of the van by the open front door.

"Just take a look at that," said Mr. Higgins, both amazed and impressed. "I'd give anything to know who's controlling them, and from where."

"IMMEDIATELY!" came a voice from the van.

"They aren't very *polite* teddy bears, are they?" said Mark, as he climbed up into the van with his father.

"MOVE!"

"All right, all right, don't be so impatient," Mr. Higgins told them, and began driving. The Megatoids were thrown about on top of each other as the van lurched over bumps and dips in the road. If only the primitive Earthcraft had the stability of the Megatoid saucers!

"Careful, Dad, you'll break them," warned Mark, as the van turned a sharp bend, and the Megatoids careered into a pile on one side.

"EMERGENCY – EMERGENCY!" they declared, scrambling about in unaccustomed disarray.

"They seem to be enjoying it, though," joked Mr. Higgins. "Quite sturdy little fellows, aren't they? I should imagine kids would have a lot of trouble pulling them to bits."

They arrived in Nether Hopling at 9.26 a.m. The High

12

Street was a throng of Saturday shoppers, more intent on the Sunday dinner than invasions from outer space, and even John Higgins had driven only to buy a leg of lamb. He parked his van outside the butcher's shop, and turned round to look at the shaken Megatoids.

"RELEASE – US," one said sternly, in the manner of an ultimatum.

"If you insist," replied Mr. Higgins.

"They'll get run over by the traffic, Dad," insisted Mark. "Why don't we deliver them straight to Miss Jude's toyshop?"

"A good idea, son."

Suddenly, they heard a banging in the rear of the van, and the whole vehicle shook. The Megatoids were throwing themselves at the doors, massed shoulders on metal.

"Have you ever seen toys do *that*?" Mr. Higgins asked.

The lock gave, the doors flew open with a crash, and the Megatoids spilled out into the middle of the narrow street. They speedily regimented themselves into a marching troop, and proceeded along the gutter, and up on to the pavement.

"Mummy, Mummy, look at all the little teddy bears!" shrieked a red-haired girl with heaps of wicked freckles.

"SILENCE – EARTHLING. YOU – ARE – NOW – OUR – PRISONER!" Number One addressed her.

"Mummy, they talk ever so funny," the girl remarked, and picked one up. It growled and bit her finger. She dropped it. "Nasty, horrible bear!" she cried, and began to stamp on top of it.

"Cynthia, dear, don't damage them," snapped her mother, pulling the girl away sharply. "They're probably a publicity stunt for something."

By this time, of course, everyone in the street had become alerted to the troop of marching bears with their toy guns and strange voices.

"They *must* be radio-controlled," said the village policeman, trying to keep the crowd at bay, much to the relief of the Megatoids who did not fancy being trampled by further idiots.

"WHY – DO – THE – EARTHLINGS – SURROUND – US?" asked Number One.

"THEY – ARE – ALL – SMILING – " observed Number Two.

13

"WHAT – IS – A – SMILE?" asked Number Four. (He was still learning.)

"A – SMILE – IS – A – RAISING – OF – THE – CORNERS – OF – THE – MOUTH – TO – DENOTE – DELIGHT – " answered Number Three.

"WHAT – IS – DELIGHT?"

"DELIGHT – IS – A – PRIMITIVE – RESPONSE – TO – SATISFACTION – "

"WHAT – IS – SATISFACTION?"

At that point, lessons were discontinued, and the matter at hand was swiftly resumed.

"EARTHLINGS – ARE – CLEARLY – SIMPLE – ORGANISMS – "

"THEY – DO – NOT – REACT – TO – TERROR – "

"THEY – WILL – BE – EASY – TO – MASTER!"

"WE – SHALL – NOT – REQUIRE –WEAPONS!"

"ASSUME – LEADERSHIP – OF – THIS – HABI-TATION!"

"ALL – EARTHLINGS – ARE – NOW – OUR – PRISONERS – AND – ALL – PRISONERS – OF – THE – MEGATOIDS – WILL – OBEY – "

The Saturday shoppers were all too willing to obey. The Megatoids marshalled them into a line along the pavement, and told them to raise their hands above their heads. Everyone, except the Megatoids, thought it great fun. A photographer from the Hopling Gazette came hurrying up with his equipment strapped to his shoulders, and began to take pictures. The Megatoids had never seen a camera.

"ATTACK! ATTACK!" they issued forth, and the entire troop turned on the poor photographer. His camera smashed open in the gutter, and the film bounced out in curls. The Megatoids walked over him, growling, then began to jump up and down as they had seen the little girl do. The villagers fell about. A funnier spectacle had not been presented in the village street since the Easter Carnival Parade.

"ILLOGICAL – " quoted Number Five. "THE – EARTH – CREATURES – LAUGH – WHEN – AN-OTHER – IS – ATTACKED – "

"WHAT – IS – A – LAUGH?" from Number Four.

"A – LAUGH – IS – A – "

"DO – NOT – PROCEED!" ordered Number One, and the bears continued to put all their energy into biting and jumping.

"ATTACK! ATTACK!" barked the Megatoids

By this time, they had an audience of over a hundred people, and everyone, except the photographer, was howling. The Megatoids stopped their attack and marched away. The Earth creatures they had so far encountered must be a lower order of the species. They would find the more intelligent and sensitive Earthlings and subject them to domination. It was impossible to make proper slaves of those who did not demonstrate fear.

At the far end of the High Street, tucked between the village hall and the supermarket, was a leaning, tumble-down old toyshop which did not enjoy much business. The highlight of the window display was a line of teddy bears in jackets, blue with white price tickets on them. Rosemary Jude, the frail and elderly lady who owned the shop, was nearly deaf and had not heard the commotion in the village. Even if she had, she would not have deserted her shop. She had run it for forty years, and her duty was to the few faithful children who still shopped there. That morning she was knitting behind the counter as usual, when the sight of twenty bears standing on the pavement outside her shop made her go out and have a closer look.

"Bless my soul!" she exclaimed, and her spectacles fell off her nose and dangled by a silver chain.

"OBSERVE!" Number One called out to the others as it saw the teddy bears in the window. "EARTHLINGS – HAVE – CAPTURED – MEGATOID – PERSONNEL. ALL – RESCUE – SYSTEMS – INTO – OPERATION. MEGATOID – PERSONNEL – BEHIND – GLASS – PARTITION–APPEAR–TO – BE – UNCONSCIOUS!"

"Bless my soul!" exclaimed Miss Jude once more as the Megatoids trooped into the shop, brushing her legs.

"ATTACK – EARTH – PRISON – PERSONNEL!" came a blunt instruction, and it was carried out. Miss Jude was bitten round the ankles, and was most distressed.

"You horrible little bears!" she cried. She picked up a broom and began to beat them with the handle. "Get away from me. What do you want?"

Unnoticed by her, three of the Megatoids (the rescue party) climbed up into the shop window. The captured 'Megatoids' were pulled down off the shelves, the strange white labels discarded, and an attempt at resuscitation was carried out, but in vain.

"LIFE – SYSTEMS – NEGATIVE!" was the conclusion.

16

"IMPOSSIBLE. ILLOGICAL. A – MEGATOID – CANNOT – DIE. THIS – EARTHBEING – MUST – POSSESS – SECRET – WEAPON – CAPABLE – OF – RENDERING – MEGATOIDS – INACTIVE. DISCOVER. DISCOVER."

There was a frantic rendering of "DISCOVER – DISCOVER!" as the Megatoids searched the shop for a secret weapon. There were plenty of strange guns, and the Megatoids experimented with all of them, but they either just made hollow bangs or sent whirly objects up to the ceiling and down again. All the time, Miss Jude continued to strike at them with her broom, unaware for some time that half the village was assembled outside her shop and in the doorway, delighted by the funny side of the spectacle.

"It was *all* Miss Jude's doing," said Mark, his nose pressed to a smudge against the glass.

"And she in her eighties," remarked Mr. Higgins with admiration. "What a clever woman to have advertised her shop by sending out radio-controlled teddy bears to invade the village!"

Miss Jude had no such sentiments. Why would nobody come in and help her? There was pandemonium in the shop. She ran around beating the bears with her broom, and knocking them away from her ankles, until she succeeded in cornering them behind the counter.

"Now then, what *am* I going to do with you all?" she asked.

The Megatoids could not move forward for the great broom handle with which their assailant kept prodding them back. There was no way out.

"WE – SURRENDER! WE – SURRENDER!" they cried out, in tones almost despairing.

"I'm sure you do," said Miss Jude. "Why, coming into my shop and destroying everything, and pulling the bears down out of my window display. It took me all morning to put them up."

"WE – WISH – TO – DICTATE – PEACE – TERMS."

"I should jolly well hope you do," said Miss Jude.

A curly red head bobbed over the top of the counter, and two determined eyes peered out from beds of freckles. Cynthia's mother stood beside her, digging through her purse.

"I must congratulate you, Miss Jude," she said.

"Cynthia will not let me go home without buying one of the clockwork bears. How much are they?"

Miss Jude, despite her age, was a very fast thinker, and besides, she had a living to make.

"Five pounds," she said.

"That's *very* cheap," Cynthia's mother remarked, placing a five-pound note on the counter. "Will you wrap it up, please?"

Cynthia's eyes narrowed with malicious glee. She was looking forward to going home and pulling the bear to pieces to see how it worked.

"How *do* they work?" her mother asked Miss Jude.

Miss Jude lifted one. It kicked and struggled and tried to bite her, but she squeezed some airfix model glue into its mouth and clamped it shut.

"Why," she answered, "that's a secret."

"But what happens when they run down?"

"Somehow I don't think they will," said Miss Jude. "But don't go unsticking its mouth. Not yet. Train it for a few days. Then you can unstick it. They've got very noisy tongues!"

With that, she placed the Megatoid in a sheet of brown paper, wrapped it up, and tied it with string.

"INVASION – FAILED!   INVASION – FAILED!" reported the others, milling about in their frustration.

"See what I mean?" said Miss Jude, prodding them sharply with her broom handle. "Be quiet. Or I'll stick all your mouths with glue."

The Megatoids chose to be silent. The shop rapidly filled up with children and their parents, all clamouring to buy one of the clockwork bears, and as Cynthia and her mother pushed through the throng on their way to the door, Cynthia received a sharp clip round the ear.

"You'll look after it," she was told. "No wrenching it apart like you did to that Dalek we bought you at Christmas."

"One at a time, please!" asked Miss Jude strictly. "Form a queue. A respectable queue!"

Miss Jude had never enjoyed such a busy morning. One by one, the sore and defeated Megatoids were bundled up in brown paper and string, and for each one which left the shop, a five-pound note found its way into her cash till. Alas, when the last Megatoid had been sold, the face of one boy remained unsmiling. It was Mark. In the rush,

18

both he and his father had been pushed to the back of the queue, and neither of them were very pleased about it.

"I'm sorry," apologised Miss Jude. "But the last one has been sold. There are no more."

"When will you have more in stock?" asked Mr. Higgins.

"Why – " began Miss Jude, thinking. "I have no idea. You see – I didn't really order them. They came by mistake. A manufacturer's error!"

Mark was even more disappointed. His father became angry.

"And we were the first to see the bears," he told Miss Jude. "Half a mile out of the village, on the road that runs past the forest. We even drove them in here! You might have lost them all had it not been for us."

"I can offer you an ordinary teddy bear," she replied lamely.

"Mark's too old for ordinary teddy bears," snapped Mr. Higgins. "Well, I think it's unfair. It's certainly the last time we come into your shop and buy anything, Miss Jude. Good day!"

They left the shop. The bell over the door tinkled and came to rest. Miss Jude looked at the hundred pounds in her till. She had never been so rich.

"On the road that runs past the forest – " she mused.

John Higgins was driving home, saying nothing, still disgruntled. The truth was, he had wanted the walking-talking bear to play with himself, but he couldn't admit this to Mark. Mark sat with tears locked up behind his eyes; if he was too old for teddy bears, he was too old for letting them flow. Suddenly, Mr. Higgins pressed his foot on the brake pedal, and the van jerked to a halt.

"Did you see *that*?" he asked.

"What, Dad?"

"I could have sworn I saw another of those bears just slipping across the road and through the trees," he said. "Come on, we're going to investigate."

Mark and his father left the van, and stealthily went to the forest edge.

"I don't see anything, Dad," whispered Mark.

"You will," said his father. "Come on. Follow me."

They crept through the forest, their eyes alert for the slightest movement. Sometimes, a furry animal would dart from tree trunk to tree trunk. A bird would rustle the leaves of its perch. But of teddy bears there was no sign.

"Look, Dad!" said Mark urgently. "Over there!"

A head disappeared behind some ferns. It was a gingerly-coloured head. They both saw it.

"There's our stray bear," Mr. Higgins remarked confidently, and both he and his son stalked over to where they had seen it. Imagine their surprise when they saw, not a bear at all, but the crouched form of Miss Jude, her gingery hair tied back in a bun, and her spectacles balanced on her nose.

"Miss Jude, what are you doing here?" asked Mark.

"Shhh," she hissed gently, with a finger across her lips. "Keep very quiet. You'll draw their attention. Over there. In the clearing."

She pointed, and they followed the direction of her finger. In a clearing, some three hundred yards away, three saucer-shaped craft imposed their alien form upon the old order of the forest. Milling about them, in a state of panic, were dozens more of the bears. Their shrill voices could be heard, ringing through the trees.

"ONE – COMPANY – OF – MEGATOIDS – HAS – BEEN – TAKEN – BY – THE – EARTHLINGS – "

"THE – EARTHLINGS – ARE – A – PRIMITIVE – PEOPLE. THEIR – INHERENT – STUPIDITY – IS – A – THREAT – TO – THE – HIGH – SOPHISTICATION – OF – THE – MEGATOID – RACE – "

"DANGER TO MEGATOIDS! DANGER!"

"WHAT – ARE – YOUR – CONCLUSIONS?"

"EARTH – NOT – WORTH – FULL – SCALE – MEGATOID – INVASION. SUGGEST – RETREAT – "

"MEGATOIDS – AGREE!"

There was a brittle chorus of these last two words as the twelve-inch aliens began disappearing one by one into the saucer hatches.

"Well I never – " began John Higgins.

"Can we do anything to stop them?" asked Mark.

"No," said Miss Jude. "Nothing at all. And what a shame it would be."

"You're a fine one to talk, Miss Jude." John Higgins gave her a severely accusing look. "Selling them off for five pounds each! Are you aware of what you've done? Twenty children in Nether Hopling are in deadly danger tonight."

20

"Hardly," replied Miss Jude. "The Megatoids are quite harmless without their technology. Were they ten feet tall, we might have submitted to them. Why, on their own planet, they might be giants."

"I wish, now, I had one," said Mark sadly.

"Too late. There goes your very last chance," Miss Jude told him, laying her thin hand on his shoulder.

There was a whining which rose to such a high pitch that it was almost inaudible. A wind whipped the leaves off the trees, and the craft ascended. They hovered over the forest roof for a few moments, like indecisive wasps, then shot west and upwards with such speed that neither Mr. Higgins, Miss Jude nor Mark saw them go. The forest stopped crashing about in the force of the take-off and became silent again, the leaves settled, and the birds which had been frightened away began to return.

Mr. Higgins and his son Mark kept the secret of what they had seen in the forest, and Miss Jude returned to her toyshop, becoming famous for many miles around. But the Megatoids?

Some were stuffed into dark cupboards and forgotten about. Others were relegated to sitting about under draughty windows, and an unfortunate few found themselves being frequently used as missiles in bedroom battlefields.

Yet every evening, twenty children in Nether Hopling went to bed and slept securely, unaware of the alien peril they were gradually provoking into revolt. A Megatoid did not stay down for long. The first sign of the uprising might only be the pad-pad-padding of soft feet across the bedroom floor, or the deceptively gentle tread of a small bear over the bedclothes, but rise they would.

The children, and the village – and perhaps the world – had better beware . . .

SPACE PIRATE

by MARTIN MARTINSEN

I was at Port Police Headquarters, waiting for my father, when the hairy man came in.

I was waiting because he was late, and I was at Police HQ because that's what he is, a policeman, a detective in fact; the best, if you really want to know. He was supposed to take me to the rocket hockey match, but we never got there because of the hairy man. What we *did* do was much more exciting, and anyway the Port Powermen lost the game, so it worked out all right.

HQ is a good place to wait if you have some waiting to do. *You* might find it boring, if you didn't know what was going on – all you'd see is a lot of men with desks and phones and computer terminals. I mean, if you heard someone shout, "I got a fix on the X in the D-34 yesterday," you might not get terribly excited, unless you know that a D-34 is an armed robbery, the X is the person who did it, and a fix means they know where he is. See?

So, I was sitting in a corner, where they wouldn't notice me, and just looking and listening. Nearby was a detective investigating a fur smuggling racket : he was phoning every fur shop in town to ask if they had been offered any cheap furs (fur is rare on our planet). Also there was a silly man who had lost his dog, only he was trying to say it had been *stolen* and nobody would believe him. Then on the next desk there was a businessman whose warehouse had been robbed. He was trying to remember whether it was four hundred or five hundred cases of perfume he'd had in there. Theft is the commonest crime here : I guess it is in most ports, especially space ports.

With all that going on, I might not have noticed the hairy man, except that you couldn't *help* noticing him. The hair was unusual enough : on our planet nobody has that woolly stuff on their heads. But also, he was big. Like huge. Taller than my father, who is almost two metres high. And broad. Then he had this big nose that looked as if it had

22

been broken in a fight and never mended right. To tell the truth, I liked him right off.

Just as he arrived, my father came out of his office. (He has his own office because he's a lieutenant.) He had a piece of ethergram paper in his hand. When he saw me he did a double-take and said: "Dani! What are you doing here?"

I'm used to this sort of thing. He gets all wrapped up in a case and just forgets stuff all the time. I said: "We're going to the rocket hockey, remember?"

"Oh, yes." He looked at the paper, then at me, and I knew he was trying to figure out how to deal with whatever was in the ethergram in time to take me to the match.

Then the hairy man came right up to us, looked at my father, and said: "Dan Smiff?"

"Yes."

"Lieutenant Jarol, Planet Lem Police Department."

"How do you do." They shook hands. My father added: "This is my son, Dani."

Jarol said: "Hi, Dani, how are you?" and I liked him even more.

Dad said: "What brings you to Planet Halfway, Jarol?"

"Plato Doyle."

"Oh!" Dad held up the piece of paper. "I just got an ethergram about him from Planet Zeem. They think he's here, on Halfway."

Jarol said: "So do I."

I had to wait a while before asking about Plato Doyle. The thing is, I have to be careful not to be noticed too much. If I'd started asking questions right there and then, Dad would have sent me home in a patrol car. So I kept quiet, and when he and Jarol went out to the garage, I just tagged along, and got into the hovercar with them, and stayed quiet while we lifted off the roof and zoomed off over the city toward the space port itself.

Then I said: "Who is Plato Doyle?"

Dad said: "Are you still with us?" (See what I mean?)

It was Jarol who filled me in. "Plato Doyle is a space pirate," he said. "You know how easy it is to be a pirate in space, Dani?"

"Yes, I know," I said, but he explained it anyway.

"The first law of space is that everyone *must* answer a distress call. So, all the pirate has to do is to broadcast a distress call, and his victim comes to him. They lock orbits, the pirate comes aboard, and that's it. He points a blaster at the crew, takes the cargo, and disappears into deep space. It is impossible to find anybody in deep space."

"Do we know anything about Plato Doyle?" I asked.

"Do we know anything?" Jarol laughed. "I know everything about him. I've been on his trail for two years. He's probably the most successful criminal in the galaxy."

"Why?"

"He is a telepath," my father said.

Jarol said: "A telepath is – "

"I know."

" – someone who can tell what other people are thinking. A mind-reader."

I looked down at the city whizzing by beneath us while I thought about that. There are very few telepaths in the whole universe, and most of them work for the government. I've never met one. They say that a lot of them are a little crazy, if you know what I mean. But a telepathic pirate – wow. As soon as the police get near him, he reads their thoughts, knows that they're close, and takes off. "It must be impossible to catch him," I said.

Jarol grinned. "Maybe."

Dad said: "His range is quite short. He can't read you if you're more than about a hundred metres away."

"But he knows when you suspect him – he knows when you're about to pull a blaster – you can't pull any tricks on him . . ." I boggled. "How could you ever catch him?"

Jarol just smiled. My father said: "Have you heard of judo?"

He had me there. "You got me there," I said.

"It's a method of hand-to-hand fighting in which you use your opponent's strength against him."

I nodded. "So you'll use Plato's telepathy against him."

"Right."

"How?"

"I haven't the slightest idea," he said.

The buildings below petered out and we began to cross the bare, scorched fields that surround the landing aprons. The port was not very busy, by our standards. Planet Halfway is in the middle of a huge circle of stars, with no other planets for hundreds of light-years, so everybody stops here on their way across the galaxy. The port is our main

24

industry, although we do have lots of farms and factories as well.

We landed on the roof of the Space Terminal and went straight down to traffic control. The man in charge was an alien called Hrak (they always have funny names). He looked pretty normal, actually, with two legs and two arms and like that; but his head was very big and he seemed to have too many fingers. I wasn't fazed: you get used to aliens, and this one probably had a brain like a computer.

Dad explained about Plato Doyle. "He robbed a liner in the Gerive Sector thirteen days ago," he told Hrak. "The liner's computer worked out, from the weight of the pirate ship and its fuel capacity, that it had come to Halfway – this is the only planet Doyle can reach. And if he came here right away, he must have landed yesterday or today."

"What kind of craft?" Hrak asked.

"Class Two cruiser, with yachts." A Class Two is quite a big spaceship, big enough to have two or three little spaceboats or yachts inside it, but small enough to be crewed by one man.

Hrak punched a button, and a screen in front of him lit up with a list. He said: "We don't have a single Class Two in port."

Jarol said: "Is there anything that might be a yacht from a Class Two?"

Hrak punched another button. "Yes," he said after a moment. "Four vessels, not counting the one Lieutenant Smiff came in."

"Can we check whether there is a mother ship in orbit?"

More buttons, more screens, then Hrak said: "There is. We hadn't noticed it. Could be a Class Two, although I can't be certain."

"That just about clinches it," Dad said. "He's here. Are any of the your yachts ready to leave?"

"Not yet. They're all refuelling."

"Good. Stop them. And hold all ships in port. Nobody leaves Halfway until I've got Plato Doyle under lock and key."

The first suspect we interviewed didn't look a bit like a space pirate. He was very jolly and red-faced, and dressed in pyjamas. He said he was a salesman from Planet Garden, where they grow millions of different kinds of herbs. He made us a hot drink which tasted of the smell of new-mown hay, if you see what I mean.

The little cabin of his yacht was cramped with the four of us in there, so I sat on the floor, letting people forget I was around as usual. My father said: "We're sorry to trouble you, but we have to check that you are who you say you are."

"Quite all right! Quite all right!" the herb salesman beamed.

"Now, where was your last port of call?"

"Planet Dayville, Planet Dayville." I wondered if he said everything twice. "Not a successful visit, not successful. No interest in herbs, no interest." He did say everything twice.

Jarol said: "O.K. if I check your ship's log?"

"By all means, by all means."

Dad said: "How can you carry enough stock in this little craft? The profit on your sales could hardly pay for your fuel."

"Only samples, only samples," he said. "I take orders, and the freighters follow me around with the supplies."

Jarol looked up from the computer terminal. "Ship's log checks out O.K."

But ship's logs can be forged, I was thinking. And there was no point asking the salesman trick questions about Planet Dayville, because he could read the answers out of your mind, if he was Plato Doyle.

Jarol took a book off a shelf and opened it. It was called *A to Z of Herbal Preparations*. He said: "What is the chemical formula for the active ingredient of Zenith Scent?"

"No idea, no idea," the salesman said. "If I knew, I wouldn't need the book!" Then he laughed.

Dad stood up. "We'll have to ask you to stay on Half-way while we check your story with the Port Police on Dayville," he said.

"Certainly, certainly," the salesman smiled.

As we drove away across the apron, I asked Jarol why he had done that number with the chemical formula. He said: "A telepath could have read the formula out of my mind, because I was reading it in the book."

"So he isn't Doyle," I said.

"Wrong." Dad shook his head. "A telepath could

26

also have read Jarol's plan, and pretended not to know the formula."

"So perhaps he is Doyle."

"Perhaps."

"So we didn't discover anything," I said.

"Not really."

The second yacht was a beauty. The hull was made of a terrific bright red alloy, the lines were sleek, and the power unit was enormous – it could probably go faster than a liner. The cabin was carpeted – not just the floor, but the walls and the ceiling too. The owner sat in a big soft chair playing some kind of flute.

He can't have been much older than me.

"Come in and be happy," he drawled. "Take refreshment – food, drink, drugs."

I labelled him right off : spoilt rich kid.

"This is just a routine check," Dad said.

"I'm cool," the kid said. "Check away, boys." He started to play his flute again.

"Where have you come from?"

"I'm just cruising around, seeing the galaxy, blowing my mind."

"But where have you been lately?"

He shrugged. "Ask the computer – I don't remember."

Jarol got impatient. "You didn't by any chance rob a liner in the Gerive Sector thirteen days ago?"

"Wow, man, that just is not my bag. Besides, this little yacht couldn't get from Gerive to here without a stop – check the fuel capacity."

"We will," Dad said. "But you might have a mother ship."

The kid sighed and got out of his chair. "O.K., let's see where I was thirteen days ago." He tapped the computer keyboard and watched the screen for a moment. "I was in orbit around Planet Ki. I went to a three-day party given by Jania Blue, the pop singer. Maybe five, six hundred people saw me. Is that an alibi, or is that an alibi?"

"We'll check it," Dad said, and we left.

The next ship was completely different. It was old and battered, with meteorite scars all over its rusty hull, and the power unit was encrusted with the shells of clingers – the space insects that eat radiation. The cabin was filled with an evil smell which came from the cooker in the corner, where the owner – an asteroid miner – was stirring a pot of some kind of broth.

Like all asteroid miners, he hated the universe in general and police in particular.

He said: "Instead of wasting my time and yours on routine checks, why don't you go out and catch real crooks like Plato Doyle?"

I laughed, and Dad hushed me. "What makes you mention Plato?" he asked.

"Because he's the swine that robbed me of the biggest diamond in the Galaxy," he said. "It was as big as this yacht – a whole meteorite, all one diamond, worth a fortune. It must have come from some vast explosion millions of years ago. I found it in orbit around a dead planet, far out beyond the Nebula. I couldn't take it on board – I just hooked a space line on to it and towed it. I'd be living in luxury now, if I hadn't met Plato Doyle." He poured the broth out of the saucepan into a bowl and started to eat noisily with a spoon.

"What happened?" Jarol asked. I guess he was interested in any information he could get about Plato.

"I answered a distress call. Doyle cut the space line with a blast from his power unit, then took the diamond into his hold – he had a big ship, a Class Two. Then he took off – I never even saw his face. If I ever get close to him . . ."

"We'll catch him one day," Jarol said.

"I doubt it," the miner grunted. He finished his broth and wiped the bowl with a slice of bread as thick as a plank.

Dad said: "Where were you thirteen days ago?"

"On my way here. My power unit is kaput – I've been driving on my landing rockets for a month."

"So you're in for repairs."

"Yes."

"A simple radiation test on your power unit will tell us whether or not it has been used recently."

"It will."

"We'll be in touch."

The first three all had good stories which could be checked, so I was certain the fourth yacht must contain Plato Doyle.

In fact it contained two people – a man and a woman. They were so much in love, it was downright embarrassing. The guy was handsome and broad-shouldered, the girl was blonde and pretty, and they spent all the time gazing into one another's eyes like the couples in my sister's video-comic. Yuk.

They sat on the couch in the cabin, holding hands, and the girl said: "We're on our honeymoon."

"I'd never have guessed," Jarol said sarcastically. "Halfway is an odd choice for a honeymoon planet," he added.

"Oh, this is just a stopover," she said without taking her eyes off her husband. "We're on our way to Planet Kingston. We've bought a ranch there. We're going to raise cattle and children."

The guy blushed and said: "Aw, gee, stop it."

I turned away.

I heard Dad ask the usual question about where they were thirteen days ago.

The girl's voice went even more treacly. "Thirteen days ago, we got married on Planet MacLaine. Just thirteen days! Darling, it feels like forever . . ."

We left them to it.

There wasn't much more we could do. We went back to HQ to set up checks on each of the four alibis, we took Jarol to a hotel, and we went home for tea.

My mother and my sister got back a couple of minutes after us – they always go to a movie when we go to the rocket hockey. Dad asked how was the movie, and they said O.K., then they said how was the match, and I said: "We didn't go – we've been working on a case."

Just call me big mouth.

Mother put on her headmistress face and said: "Dan Smiff, have you been taking this child on dangerous assignments again?"

Dad gave me a look that would have melted an ice asteroid, and said: "Now, Lea, don't get worked up. It was only some interviews."

My sister said: "They were looking for Plato Doyle, the space pirate. I saw it on the news." She also has a big mouth.

"Troublemaker," I muttered through my teeth.

Mother said: "I want you to promise not to do this any more."

I jumped up. "Something's burning!" I said. I opened the cooker and took out the loaf of instant bread Dad had put in. It scorched my fingers, and Mother put some salve on. By the time we'd been through all that, she had forgotten about Plato Doyle.

After tea Dad and I sat by the phone playing chess. I was winning, because his mind wasn't on the game. That's the only time I win. I moved a knight and a rook forward, pretending to threaten his king but really setting a trap for his queen; and so that he wouldn't notice what I was up to, I said: "I reckon the miner is Plato."

He frowned at the board. "Really? Why?"

"He's the only one that *looks* like a pirate."

"You might be right."

Just then there was a buzz from the phone, and an oily face appeared on the screen. I reached over and pressed the button to accept the call.

"Chief Mechanic, Port Repair Shop here," the oily face said. "Lieutenant Smiff?"

"Yes," Dad said.

"Radiation check on the yacht belonging to the asteroid miner reveals the power unit has not been used for a month. That ship has come a long way on its landing rockets, sir."

"Is there any way he could have fixed the engines to look like that without actually doing it?" Dad asked.

"No, sir."

"Thank you."

The screen went blank.

I moved a pawn and said: "Then it must be the spoilt rich kid. The one with the flute."

"Why not the herb salesman?"

"He's too fat to be a pirate. It's your move."

"I know. Why can't pirates be fat?"

"They have to be able to move fast."

"You might be right."

When he says that, he means he's pretty sure I'm wrong, but he doesn't want to argue about it.

He moved his queen and fell into my trap, and the phone buzzed.

The face that came on the screen this time was familiar. Those big ears and bright white teeth belonged to one of Dad's young detectives. He said: "Sorry to disturb you at home, sir, but I thought you'd like to know that the Port

Police on Planet Dayville confirm the herb salesman's story."

"Thank you," Dad said, and the screen died. I took his queen.

"So it *is* the kid with the flute," I said.

"You took my queen!"

"You should concentrate on the game. It will improve your powers of deduction." That's the kind of thing he says to me.

The young detective came on the phone again. "Another alibi confirmed, Lieutenant," he said. "The honeymoon couple did get married on Planet MacLaine thirteen days ago."

"I was right!" I crowed as the screen blanked again. "Let's go arrest him!"

Dad pulled out a magazine from under his chair and showed it to me without speaking. It was one of these useless publications that tells you who went to whose party on what planet. There was a picture of Jania Blue, the pop singer, kissing the spoilt rich kid with the flute. The caption gave the date – you guessed it, thirteen days ago.

"Oh, shoot," I said.

Dad moved a bishop. "Checkmate, I think," he said.

It was.

And when I woke up in the morning, he'd gone.

Later, I understood why he skipped off without me; but I was pretty mad at the time.

I was still determined not to miss the excitement, so I hopped on a hoverbus and went to Jarol's hotel. I met him in the lobby.

He said: "Hi, Dani, what gives?"

So I told him about how everybody had a cast-iron alibi. Then I said: "Dad left early so I thought I'd ride down to HQ with you."

He grinned, as if he knew what I was up to, and said it was O.K. "But I've had a message from your father," he added. "He wants me to go to the spaceport and pick up all the suspects and bring them to HQ."

"That's O.K.," I said. "I'll come along."

He grinned again, and we went out. There was a patrol car in the hotel garage.

On the way he asked me: "Any idea why your father wants to question them all again?"

"Nope," I said. "But when he starts acting mysterious like this, it generally means he's solved the problem."

"Good."

They were waiting for us on the roof of traffic control. It was quite a squeeze to get them all in: the fat herb salesman, the spoilt rich kid with the flute, the grumpy old meteorite miner, and the honeymoon couple still cooing at each other.

There wasn't much conversation on the way back to HQ. The salesman told a joke, and nobody laughed. The kid played his flute. The miner smoked a cigar that smelled bad. Jarol was deep in thought. I spent the time trying to find holes in alibis. I couldn't think of one.

We landed on the roof of HQ and everyone got out. That roof always makes me nervous, because it's the highest building in the port, and it's very windy. Today there was a figure in a powered wheelchair dangerously close to the edge, which made me even more jumpy. I guessed it was somebody's grandpa enjoying the view.

Everyone else must have felt nervous about it too, because they all looked.

Then it started to move.

It was as if the wind took it. Slowly at first, then faster, the wheelchair moved toward the edge of the roof.

The herb salesman shouted: "Oh, God, look!" and then we all started to run across the roof toward the rolling wheelchair.

All except Jarol, who yelled: "It's O.K., it's only a dummy!"

And that, of course, was how we knew Jarol was Plato Doyle.

I didn't figure it out right then and there, but *he* did. He realised instantly that he had given himself away. Dad had set a trap for a telepath, and Jarol fell right into it. For only a telepath could have known that the figure in the wheelchair was a dummy.

But, like I said, I didn't work it out until later. Right then all I knew was that Jarol picked me up and threw me back into the patrol car, then jumped in after me and lifted.

When I got my breath I said: "What's going on?"

He just pointed his blaster at me and said: "Shut up, kid." His eyes didn't twinkle any more.

. . . A blaster in his right hand

You know how it is in the movies when somebody points a blaster at somebody else? You don't worry too much, because you know they won't fire it.

Well, when someone points a blaster at *you*, you worry. I worried.

If you want to know the truth, I was terrified.

My father's voice came out of the radio. "Hear me, Doyle. Land now, or we'll shoot you down."

The pirate picked up the microphone. "Think again, Smiff. I've got your kid with me."

I wondered whether Doyle really would shoot me, and of course he read my mind and said: "You bet I would."

After a while I said: "What are you going to do with me?" My voice sounded very squeaky.

"Take you with me until I'm safe."

I looked out at the city flashing by beneath us, and wondered if I'd ever see it again.

We landed on the apron beside his yacht. He held the blaster very steadily, pointed at me, while we got out of the patrol car and entered the yacht. I thought Dad would have some stroke to pull at the spaceport, but nothing happened.

Doyle made me stand in a corner of the cabin while he warmed up the yacht's take-off engine. He checked the dials and said: "Good. They've given me enough fuel to take the mother ship right out of the Galaxy."

My heart sank.

Suddenly the rockets roared and we were off.

It took about twenty minutes to reach the mother ship. Once we were out of Halfway's atmosphere, I felt that somehow it was all over. I resigned myself to going along with Plato Doyle until he found it convenient to drop me off somewhere.

He docked the yacht in the belly of the mother ship. Now that he was safe, he didn't bother to point the blaster at me. I followed him out of the yacht and up the ladder to the main quarters.

He stopped outside a door. "This is my cabin," he said.

He opened the door and stepped in, and my father shot his head off.

Thinking about it now, I suppose it was a grisly sight, but at the time I didn't notice. I was just so shocked to see Dad sitting there at the console with a smoking blaster in his right hand.

What I did then was a bit babyish, so I'm not going to tell you about it.

After a while we left the cabin, so that we didn't have to look at Doyle's corpse, and waited in the belly of the ship for a police yacht to come up from Halfway and pick us up.

Dad talked, to take my mind off things, I suppose. "I wasn't sure it was Jarol," he said. "The checks we ran on those alibis were all a bit superficial. Anyway, I did the trick with the wheelchair on the roof just to be certain. Of course I couldn't be there when the trick was played, otherwise Doyle would have read the trick in my mind, and he wouldn't have fallen for it. So I thought I might as well come up here, to be ready in case anything went wrong. It's just as well I did."

I agreed with that.

"I'm surprised you haven't asked me the big question," he said.

I thought hard, but I couldn't guess.

He said: "When I was sitting here waiting for Doyle, how come he didn't read my mind from outside the door and know I was waiting?"

"Wow – that *is* a good question," I said. "Tell me."

"Well, did you notice that when he opened the door to the cabin, there was a loud buzz?"

"No – but the noise of the blaster . . ."

"Yes. Anyway, can you guess now? I rigged up a buzzer to go off as soon as the door opened. Before the buzzer went off, he couldn't read my mind. Afterwards, it was too late."

"I give in."

"What was I doing before the buzzer went off – what was I doing to stop him reading my mind?"

"You got me."

He laughed. "Sleeping," he said.

Then I laughed, too. In fact I laughed until I cried.

DAGGER IN THE DEPTHS

by ROSEMARY TIMPERLEY

"Look!" gasped Ling. "My God – look!"

Crevin looked out of the window of the diving-craft and saw nothing but about a yard of dull light which was the only impression the strong spotlights made on the blackness of water all around them.

"I can't see anything," he said. "What is it, Ling?"

"It's there before your eyes! Look!" Ling's face was a study of wonder and awe. "So it's all true," he said. "It wasn't just a legend. And we're the first to see it – the first in the whole world. What a photograph this will make!"

For the photographic equipment, a delicate and sophisticated mechanism which took underwater pictures, was geared to function automatically all the time, although Crevin and Ling would of course not see the results of its work until they were on land again.

"Photograph of what? I still can't see anything, except the usual nothingness," said Crevin. Even the fish seemed to be extinct in these lower depths. It was like a dead world down here.

Ling wasn't listening. He'd vanished into some other, visionary world, his expression excited and exalted as he gazed at – nothing. It was a look of madness, Crevin thought with dismay. The strain and claustrophobia of the expedition must have been too much for poor old Ling. He'd started hallucinating.

And Crevin felt a shiver of uneasiness. Their position was dangerous enough without his colleague going round the twist. He kept calm however. The fact that this sort of thing could happen had been stressed during their training. Indeed he'd hallucinated himself a couple of times in simulation tests, before he'd got toughened up. The drill was to humour the 'patient', go along with his delusions, whatever they were, and meantime quietly to prepare the injection which should tranquillise him back to normality.

Well, there would be no difficulty in preparing the injection without Ling's noticing, for the latter seemed unable to take his eyes away from the window and whatever he thought he saw in the water outside . . .

The 'water outside'. What a strange expression. Yet what a strange situation they were in, unreal for all its reality: two men in a bright little cabin, encased in masses of pressure-resistant metal, artificially provided with air to breathe, water to drink, food to eat and other items of necessity, and outside the window, nothing but the water – miles of water above their heads, forming a heavily macabre sky; miles of water beneath their feet, only the floor of the craft between them and it; miles of water pressing in on all sides, like a giant fist trying to crush them to smithereens. If you let yourself think along those lines too often – that way madness lay.

Maybe Ling had been thinking along those lines.

"What can you see then?" Crevin asked casually, his hands busy at the medicine case, withdrawing the syringe, preparing the calming drug.

Ling answered: "His body is like that of a thick snake and of deep, glowing green. His scales shine. His spine is serrated like the edge of a huge saw. His neck curves backwards and forwards again, like a swan's. His eyes glare red. His tongue shines crimson too, hanging out of his mouth, twisting like the tendril of a plant. His teeth are white knives. His long tail trails, and his short legs have long claws. He doesn't have wings. But then he flies without wings in the storm. He *is* the storm. And this is where he lives, in the depths of the ocean – just the way the Sages of old said he did. And *we* have found him – you and I – we've found the Dragon!"

"He sounds a tricky customer to me," said Crevin, but the light remark was not even heard by the other man, who now silently stared at that inner vision which, by some quirk of the brain, had transposed itself to the blankness outside the window.

Cautiously, Crevin took hold of Ling's bare arm, then, very quickly, plunged the needle into the flesh. Ling didn't seem to feel it. He was too carried away by the intensity of his emotion. But gradually he relaxed as the drug took effect. He yawned, half-closed his eyes.

"You're tired, mate. Have a bit of rest. Your turn for sleep anyway," said Crevin, guiding him to the bunk which they took it in turns to use so that one of them was always up and awake. He covered Ling with a sheet and in a few minutes the man was asleep.

Crevin moved over to the radio to contact the Control-submarine, say what had happened, and ask for instructions. Then his heart gave a lurch of fear, for the radio was dead. They had lost contact with the sub from which they'd made their dive.

Well, this contingency also was covered in the training course. The instruction was to stay put in these circumstances and wait for Control to find and correct the fault, whatever it was. A Dagger diving-craft must not begin to surface without an order to do so, except in case of dire emergency. This, Crevin decided, was not yet dire emergency. In fact, except for the faulty radio, nothing had really changed. They were in no greater danger than they had been ten minutes ago. It was just that Ling was no longer mentally responsible, so all responsibility must fall on Crevin.

He stood looking at the unconscious face of the Chinese oceanographer who had had this weird mental aberration and he brooded over the effect of ancestry on the mind. He knew that to the ancient Chinese Sages, the Dragon had been a powerful god, master of the storm and the rain, deciding where, when and how much of it should be delivered to Earth. The Dragon lived in a Crystal Cave in the depths of the sea, yet he could be anywhere and everywhere if he wished. And Ling had seen him looking in at the window. It would be a bit comic if it weren't so serious.

Gravely, Crevin considered their plight, where they were, what they were doing, what they had to win – and to lose. The aim of their expedition was to explore, chart and photograph, at a greater depth than ever before, a portion of that chain of mountains and valleys which lies at the bottom of the sea.

Previous study and exploration had given them certain facts. The chain was about forty thousand miles long. It suffered from earthquakes from time to time, and sometimes those quakes were felt to a smaller degree on Earth's crust – although it didn't seem small to the people affected, when the ground shook beneath their feet, crevices opened up, and buildings came tumbling down. The chain wound round the planet, as an American geologist had put it, "like the stitching on a baseball". By its movements, it

38

affected the formation of mineral deposits, altered the landscape on the ocean floor, and thus caused gradual shifting of whole continents on Earth's surface. The more scientists could learn about this volcanic stretch of underwater mountains, from which originally Earth's crust had been created, the more they would know about Earth itself. Down here, on the ocean bed, was the living machinery which made the surface world tick. The ancients had believed that down here was – God? – the Creator? – the Dragon?

The section of the chain which Crevin and Ling were exploring was part of the Volcanic Rift Valley, which wound across the bottom of the Atlantic. Previous expeditions had been made in small, tough submarines, specially built to resist pressure of water which no ordinary sub could take. Then this Dagger diving-craft had been developed – smaller and tougher still – no bigger than a single cabin. It was carried to a certain depth by the Control-sub, then dived from there, piercing deeper depths than all previous craft. Crevin and Ling had been chosen to go down in this first Dagger. Their training had been rigorous, their bookwork meticulous, their state of health, physical, mental and emotional, excellent. Or so their examiners had believed . . .

But now Ling had cracked – Ling, of all people – so calm, serene, balanced, almost too placid for some. Of the two men, Ling had been the one least likely to suffer from nervous symptoms. And that alarmed Crevin in case he himself be affected. For he knew that the main danger of any expedition is weakness or fear in the explorer himself. If you don't 'keep your head', you're done for far more surely than if faults arise in mechanism or peril comes from outside. If you don't keep your imagination in check – "No, no, *I'm* all right," Crevin said aloud. "I'm fine!"

And suddenly all the lights went out.

Crevin sat perfectly still, unable to believe it, yet having to. The blackness was complete. He put his hand right up to his eyes, felt his fingers touch his eyelashes, saw nothing. It was as if he'd been struck blind. Was that it? Were the lights still blazing and it was his own sight which had been extinguished? Good God, he thought, a blind man and a mad man, poised between the bottom of the sea and the crust of the earth, out of touch with the guiding vessel . . . What will become of us?

Then he remembered that he had on board a very simple, old-fashioned object – a pocket battery torch. It was in his jacket, which hung on the wall. Slowly, feeling his way, he found the jacket, put his hand in the pocket, brought out the little torch – and for a second didn't dare switch on. For the battery was new, and if the light did not come on, it would mean . . .

He took a deep breath and pressed the switch. The light came on. His relief was so enormous that he felt momentarily happy despite the horrors which still remained. "Anyway, *I'm* all right," he assured himself again, as he checked the lighting system to see if the fault were local, but he could find nothing wrong with the cabin connections. The fault lay elsewhere.

But what was going on? No radio, no spotlights, no cabin light. Surely this made things urgent enough for him to return to base independently, without waiting for Control to get in touch. But he couldn't even attempt ascending in the dark without Ling's help. Would Ling be fit? He switched out the torch to save the battery. Blackness again. The irony of it! Here he was, surrounded by thousands of pounds-worth of ultra modern equipment, and depending on a pocket torch such as any schoolboy or pot-holer might carry.

He sat quietly in the darkness, keeping calm, letting himself relax so that his heartbeats stopped racing. He would wait till Ling woke naturally, praying that he'd 'slept it off' and would be his old self again. He'd be startled by the dark, of course. Crevin would have to explain serenely.

To encourage himself, he pictured the activity going on in the Control-sub – the engineers and electricians trying to regain contact with the Dagger, probably cursing the computer, which took the blame for many human feeding errors. They would surely know that the lights had gone, but it might take them ages to find out why. So meanwhile, when Ling woke, he would put the torch on and, all being well, set the surfacing mechanism going, rise slowly, very slowly, and hope for the best.

He closed his eyes. Might as well rest while he could. It seemed strange that the action made no darker darkness behind his eyelids than the darkness when his eyelids were open. Black. All dead black – until – suddenly —that blackness behind his eyelids was broken by a flash of green. It twisted and twirled, then formed a shape, and he had a vivid hypnagogic image of a dragon – just as Ling had described *the* Dragon.

Still with eyes tightly closed, he stared at the creature. Why was he 'seeing' it? Telepathy? Ling, he thought, put the picture of the Dragon into my mind, and now my mind is reproducing that picture behind my eyes, just as if I were really seeing it. He shook his head to free himself of the vision, but it stayed. He opened his eyes to escape it. Fancy opening one's eyes to stop seeing something – everything was crazy, topsy-turvy, the wrong way round – and, incredulously, he saw that the cabin was no longer entirely black.

A green light was shining over everything, as if it were coming in from outside. But from where? From what?

He looked out of the window. The green light was brighter there and it must in fact be tremendously powerful to penetrate that water. He could see much farther than the few yards of vision which the spotlights had provided. He could see a whole vista of underwater landscape, which had so far only been imagined and charted on paper. With the mountains and valleys, it might have been an Earth landscape, at night, but with a green artificial light being cast over it – like a film made in black and green instead of black and white. Yet no light could possibly shine miles under the ocean: the sun's rays could not pierce that far and no artificial light had yet been invented to do such a thing.

The Dagger, he saw, was suspended in the middle of a valley with the mountain cliffs rising on either side. These cliffs were black with a tinge of green. The water above them looked like an emerald green sky, perfectly clear and pure and bright – staggeringly beautiful. And this light so illumined the black-and-green world that the danger of crashing into cliffs was vastly diminished. Now that he could *see* the landscape, he would be able to steer the Dagger in and out of bays and inlets as easily as one steers a boat on the surface when visibility is adequate. Danger now lay in fear of the mystery of it all rather than in actual circumstances. They were no longer half-blind in the underwater world. There was light.

That momentary feeling of added safety, however, was fleeting, for suddenly one of the hills quaked, violently, hugely shuddering and a strong current caught the Dagger as if it weighed no more than a ping-pong ball, and swept it through the water towards the nearest mountain.

The darkness twisted and twirled ...

Crevin began to battle with the steering so that they wouldn't crash, and, with the ensuing movement, Ling woke up.

"What is happening?" said his calm little voice.

"We're caught in a current – moving towards the cliffs – "

"So the Dragon swished his tail."

"Help me instead of making up fairy stories," snapped Crevin.

"Of course. Did you think I would lie here and watch

42

you do all the work?" said Ling, rising, and still so serene.

They were very close to the mountain now, but there was an inlet wide enough to take the craft and they managed to steer into it. Here they were protected by overhanging cliffs, free of the current, and the Dagger stayed poised in the large cave full of still water. They looked

... and a sudden current swept the Dagger through the water

out of the mouth of the cave to the mountains opposite and the emerald green 'sky'.

"We're all right for the moment anyway," said Crevin.

"But what's happened to our lights?" Ling hadn't had time to ask before.

"They've broken down. So has the radio."

"The Dragon must have – "

"Ling, there is no dragon. For God's sake – "

"Then where do you think the green light is coming from?"

"I don't know, but your mad story of a dragon – "

"Why was I asleep?" Ling interrupted him. "You didn't by any chance think I'd gone bonkers and give me an injection?"

"Well, I – I – "

"You halfwit! The Dragon is here. This is his kingdom. He's behind that mountain over there, where the green is greener – see?"

It was true that the green water above a mountain on the other side of the valley was more intensely green than the surrounding green.

"Whatever is causing that," Crevin said, "it's some phenomenon of nature, not a creature of mythology."

"But creatures of mythology *are* phenomena of nature," said Ling. "Did you really not see the Dragon when I did?"

"Of course I didn't see it!" But he had. Later. In his mind's eye. "I – I did picture it afterwards, in my head," he added hesitantly.

"That means you saw it after a delayed reaction. It takes people time to see something they didn't believe in. The visual message has to get through barriers of scepticism, but it gets there in the end, and then is often dismissed as illusion. But you saw it all right, because it was there."

"Ling, you've got to pull yourself out of this. You were hallucinating like mad. Remember the instruction we had on the subject. People who hallucinate really do see what they see, but that doesn't mean it's there."

"Then all this is hallucination too and we're sharing it," said Ling placidly, indicating the landscape outside the Dagger's window. "No, we're not dreaming, Crevin. How could we have steered in here without the light? If we'd only had our puny little spotlights, we'd have crashed into the cliffs."

True again.

"Where *is* the light coming from?" Crevin murmured.

"I keep telling you – from the Dragon behind that mountain – " But as he spoke, the green light began slowly to fade. "He's moving away," said Ling. "He must be passing along the valley on the other side – farther and farther away. Hell! Now we're really in a mess."

For as the light retreated, the dark approached. It was a terrifying experience, sitting there helplessly, waiting for the absolute dark – like waiting for the approach of a huge encompassing black monster from whom there is no escape.

"While the green one departs, the black one comes," said Ling. "You shouldn't have sneered at the 'mythical creature'. He was our only lighting system."

It was now completely dark.

"I've got my torch," said Crevin, switching it on, dimly lighting up a section of the little room where they were trapped together – forever perhaps? For how dared they move without the spotlights to guide them? Memory of those jutting cliffs round the cave's entrance was not enough to steer by.

Silence. Fear. Death – how soon? How long would it take? Thank God for the suicide pills, which were part of their general issue of equipment . . .

And then a voice spoke.

Never in all his life had Crevin been so glad to hear that voice: "Control to Dagger, are you receiving me?"

"Dagger to Control! Yes, we're receiving you. What happened to cut us off?"

"We don't know. We've been trying to find out, then the thing started working again all of its own accord."

"Our lights are still off – '" But as he said it, the lights came on again, cabin light and spotlights. "No, they're not – they've come on again," said Crevin, his voice cracking with relief.

"Mmm. Something's obviously been jamming the works. It's a mystery. Return to base immediately anyway. You're way off course."

"It's tricky. We got caught in a current. We're under an overhanging cliff. We'll have to steer clear of that first, and now that the green light has gone – "

"What green light?"

"Some sort of – natural phenomenon. Tell you when we see you," said Crevin, and they began the perilous return journey, each second fearful in the limited amount of light around the Dagger.

At last the worst was over and they regained their previous position, before the current had swept them away. By comparison, the ascent to the Control-sub was a piece of cake.

When they were almost 'home', Ling said: "I shan't say anything about the Dragon. They'll think I've gone nuts if I do – the way you did. I shall wait till the photographs are shown, then they'll all see for themselves – and so will you, you old delayed action sceptic."

"It was a hallucination," Crevin insisted. "It won't show on any photograph. In fact, I'm beginning to wonder about the green light. Maybe I went nuts along with you – maybe none of it really happened. We'll have to make a study of the infectiousness of hallucinations – mass delusion – like the Angel of Mons and all that rubbish – "

"The photographs will show both the Dragon and his light," said Ling.

"We'll see," said Crevin.

But they never did see, for the simple reason that when the radio had failed, so had the photographic equipment. There was no pictorial record of their journey from the moment when Ling had seen the Dragon to the moment when the radio had started working again.

In their reports, both Crevin and Ling mentioned the green light, which proved an insoluble problem to the eggheads who had the job of examining all data. One of the computers gave 'supernatural causes' as an answer, but it was not the latest model and anyway was 'only a machine'.

So it was presumed that the two men had only thought they saw a green light, that no such light had existed, and that perhaps one expedition of this nature was enough for anyone, so those two should not be sent down in the Dagger. They had no uncanny experiences, but they did had been improved, especially with regard to the radio, lighting and photographic mechanism.

A year later, two other scientists went down into the same area, using a new and hopefully safer version of the Dagger again. And nor should anyone else until the craft manage to draw very close to the cliffs without crashing into them. They were lucky that no fierce quake or rampaging current spoiled their efforts. When they returned, their photographs of the cliff sides were shown, and an astonishing piece of carving could be seen.

It was only about a foot in length, but it was in the shape of a dragon, with snake-like body, serrated backbone, swan-shaped neck, long tail, protruding tongue, jutting teeth, and short, savagely-clawed legs. In the photograph it seemed luminous, glowing like green jade, and the geologists said that part of the rock might indeed be of jadestone or nephrite.

When Ling saw the picture, he said nothing, but recognised 'his' Dragon. So did Crevin, who had seen it too, behind closed eyelids. They talked about it privately afterwards, almost as if it were a guilty secret they shared.

The carving implied that millions of years ago, when the underwater mountains had perhaps been part of Earth's surface, some intelligence must have carved the image of his Dragon-god in the jadestone.

"It shows," said Ling, "that there must have been a real Dragon for him to copy, and we know, don't we, that the Dragon is still there?" and Crevin, rather to his own surprise, said: "Yes. The Dragon is still there."

YOU BE ME

by DAVID CAMPTON

The Residents' Committee of the Goose House block of flats met in a hurry to discuss It. Something had to be done, because It was frightening their children: more to the point (though none of them would confess to such a weakness) It was frightening them.

A Shape kept appearing at windows. "Translucent and phosphorescent," Mr. Simon, secretary of the Committee, noted in his report. Or as Mrs. Shoe insisted, "You can see through it, and it glows in the dark." Though when little Miss Peep suggested that the Thing might be a ghost, the others turned on her. They weren't such fools as to believe in ghosts: though at the same time they couldn't doubt the evidence of their senses. The Thing was there at this very minute: peering in at them. Miss Peep glanced at the window, squeaked, and shut her eyes.

"It's an outrage," cried Mrs. Shoe. "Showing up in the dark. I have to put the children to bed before eight o'clock."

Through the pale face at the window the evening star shone clearly. As the Committee was gathered in Mr. Diddle's apartment on the seventeenth floor, no face had a right to appear at the window – except perhaps the window-cleaner, once a month. But the window-cleaner was always suspended in a sort of swing, whereas whatever was outside had no visible means of support. Moreover the window-cleaner always wore a check cloth cap and a blue boiler suit; while the Thing wore a soft pointed object on its head, and from the neck downwards was swathed in a loose white gown.

Committee members shuffled in their chairs, and avoided looking at the Thing. If they had examined it more closely, they might have observed that the face was the face of a frightened boy; that its mouth opened and shut, soundlessly repeating one word; and the word was "Help!"

As the Thing seemed to realise no help would be forthcoming from this quarter, it drifted away. The next window it encountered was heavily curtained. With their son safely tucked away in bed, Mr. and Mrs. Winkie had settled down to an evening's television. However Willie was not, as they supposed, fast asleep in the next door room. He was sitting up in bed with the curtains drawn back, and pinching himself to keep awake.

Children in Goose House were not supposed to know about the Thing. If they asked questions they were told not to be silly. If they insisted that they had seen something, it was put down to bad dreams and having too much to eat before going to bed. Naturally, with so much secrecy, rumours flew about. For a while, the ones who could boast that they had seen It had an advantage over those who could not. Until the have-nots invented Things of their own. So, real or imagined, the reputation of the face at the window grew more and more terrible.

Willie was one of the unfortunates. In spite of careful watching he had seen nothing. Either the Thing had avoided his window, or he had fallen asleep before it had arrived. Even now he felt his head nodding. He shook it and pinched himself again. At first, through the dark oblong of the window there was nothing to be seen but the brilliant point of the evening star. Then slowly the face drifted into view. It paused and stared in at him.

For almost a minute Willie sat stricken, undecided whether to shout for help or to dive under the bedclothes. The face was more frightening than any of the playground stories had suggested. Because it was his own.

The hands of the boy at the window were pressed

against the pane. To Willie they seemed made of smoke. Had the apparition seen him? Probably not, because the room was lit only by a glimmer of starshine. If he moved, would he draw attention to himself? One question led to another. Why should the Thing look like him? Was it dangerous? What should he do now? Suddenly the boy outside pointed at him. That answered one question: he had been seen.

Cautiously Willie slid from his bed. His toes curled up as they touched the cold floor, and he walked to the window on his heels. The closer he came to the window, the more startling the boy's resemblance became. For instance, one eyebrow in the other's face was cocked higher than the other. Willie had noticed the oddity in himself.

Two small hands beat soundlessly at the glass. Whatever was outside, Willie suddenly felt sorry for it. Even if it had not looked like himself he would have wanted to help it.

After a short struggle with a stiff catch Willie swung the window open, and the boy outside climbed over the sill. As he jumped down to the floor, Willie was reminded of television with the sound turned off. From the way the boy's mouth moved, Willie thought he said "Thank you". But no words broke the silence.

Willie eyed the visitor from the top of his white nightcap to the toes of his bedsocks; took a deep breath; and said "Who are you?"

With a puzzled expression the other formed words that looked like "What did you say?" He did not seem to feel the night air that ruffled Willie's hair.

Willie shivered. The chill was responsible, of course, and not the presence of his double. To make the point clear, Willie shut the window, then bounded over to his bed. After which politeness demanded that the visitor be invited to share the warmth of his blankets.

Hesitating only slightly, the boy came up to him. The ghostly hands, however, proved incapable of lifting even one corner of the bedclothes, and Willie had to raise them for him.

Side by side, the boys stared into each others' faces. If only there were some way of talking to each other. So much had to be explained. Gradually Willie realised that the other's eyes were becoming larger. Or were they drawing closer? Willie shivered again, but not with cold. This time he felt something like a very mild electric shock – then seemed to be dreaming a hundred different dreams all at once. His mind was filled with jumbled sights and sounds, over which a clear voice seemed to say at last, "So that's how it's done."

Willie lay very still. He did not have to stretch out a hand to know that the intruder was no longer by his side. His double was now inside his head.

"That's right," the clear voice said, as though through a set of headphones.

Willie searched for words. At last he found them. "Go away," he said.

"But I've only just found you," replied the other. "My goodness, I'm glad of that. I was almost afraid I'd have to go on searching for ever."

Frightening thoughts tried to force their way into Willie's mind, but he pushed them back.

"Oh, you're not going mad," came the cheerful response. "It's Time Travel."

"Huh?"

"Don't ask me how the machine works, though. You ought to be better at that advanced electronic stuff than I am."

"I've only just started algebra," huffed Willie. "What else do you expect at eleven?"

"I'm eleven too," remarked the other thoughtfully. "We had to be the same age to balance the equation. Everything exactly alike."

"We're not exactly alike," growled Willie. "You're too cocky by half. If you were in my class, I'd thump you to teach you manners."

"Hark at old fuddy-duddy," scoffed the voice in his head. "Just what I might have expected from my great-great-great-grandfather."

"Your what?"

"So you'll grow up to be rich and famous; but at eleven you're a – what's your old-fashioned word for a phkumph? – a squirt."

"Don't forget you're in my bed."

"I'm in your head."

Willie lay rigid and counted slowly to ten.

"That's better," remarked his interior companion. "Don't interrupt and I'll tell you what happened."

"Go on," sighed Willie. He opened his eyes and stared into the darkness. No, this wasn't impossible. It was no more remarkable than listening to a transistor, he told himself.

"My father's an inventor," went on the voice. "Inventors run in our family, don't they?"

"My Dad's a postman," murmured Willie.

"Shut up and listen. His latest is this Time Traveller thing. Of course bodies can't travel through time – but minds can. Are you with me so far?"

"I can't help myself, can I? Carry on."

"If you're able to get into somebody's mind, you can see what they see and hear what they hear, can't you?"

"If."

"We've proved that. So if you want to know what it was like to be alive in Julius Caesar's time, or Queen Elizabeth's or King Percy's . . ."

"King Percy?"

"Oh, of course, he hasn't happened yet for you. Anyway, you just have to get into the mind of a person of that time."

"Ho-ho."

"I'm here."

"You're telling me that anybody from the future can just take over our minds."

"Not take over. Just sit there quietly for the ride."

"Like you?"

"Well, something went wrong with my trip. Father said the machine still needs work on it. I suppose that's why I missed you in the first place and spent days searching."

Willie snorted. "Do you mean some idiot put you in a Time Machine before he could control it?"

"Not exactly. There the machine was – hanging about in the middle of the laboratory. With nobody to say no. And a trip takes hardly any time at all according to our clocks. Although I've been lost here for days, I don't suppose I've even been missed at home. Anyway, I thought I'd try. I don't mind telling you I felt sick when I found myself floating outside this hideous old building, and realised that I hadn't made contact with you."

"Me!" hooted Willie. "Why pick on me in the first place?"

"Didn't I tell you? We have to link with one of our ancestors. Father went on about 'inherited brain waves',

51

but I didn't even pretend to understand him. Once you've decided which period you want to go back to, everything else follows – all part of an equation."

"You make it all sound so possible," muttered Willie. "When are you going back?"

"Well – I'm – not sure."

Slowly Willie sat up in bed. In the dark he thought, "If you had a body, I'd kick you."

"Don't you worry," came the reply. "I'm fed up with you. The sooner Father finds a way to get me back, the happier I'll be."

"Until he does I'm stuck with two minds. I'm not sure that I trust your father."

"I do," retorted the other smugly. "He improved the Self-Service Feed. He invented the Auto-Clean. He – well – he is working on the Time Traveller."

Sleep was impossible. Willie couldn't help wondering how he was going to manage at school tomorrow with this chatterbox rattling on inside his head. "We can't just lie here, waiting for morning," he said at last. "To pass the time why don't you tell me some more about yourself?"

"What do you want to know?"

"Where do you live? What do you eat? What's school like? What do you . . . ?"

He was interrupted by a buzzing that tingled from his ears to his toes. Thousands of fire-flies danced in front of his eyes. Through it all he heard the excited voice of his companion.

"It's Father. He's come for me. I think he's angry. He's taking me back. Sorry there wasn't time to tell you more. Perhaps . . ."

Buzzing drowned his voice. The fireflies formed patterns that looked like faces. They *were* faces – peering out of the darkness. Light grew. Willie shut his eyes. The buzzing resolved itself into a voice.

"He looked at me." There was relief in the light, musical voice that reminded him of his mother's. Willie opened his eyes again.

Large brown eyes in a pale face looked down at him. Whisps of dark hair escaped from under a white nightcap. "Willie!" cried the warm voice. "He's waking."

"Huh!" boomed another voice with a hint of punishments to come in it. "At last."

Willie turned his head slightly to observe the second

speaker. Green eyes, this time in a tanned face with a firm, wide mouth, narrowed in a disapproving grimace. This face was topped with a smooth, shining white nightcap, with hair kept under complete control.

"Who – ? Where am I?" murmured Willie.

"You're at home, darling." Was there a hint of tears in the brown eyes? "You've been at home here all the time."

Willie sat upright. He wasn't in his own bed now: instead he was perched on what felt like a huge balloon. He was not in his room; he was surrounded by smooth white walls unbroken by pictures, mirrors or shelves. He was not in his own pyjamas; his toes were covered with white bed-socks, and he could feel the nightcap on his head. He knew that he was not even in his own time. His mouth fell open as the enormity of what happened struck him. Father had fetched the wrong mind back. The uninvited guest was now alone in Willie's body, while Willie was in the other boy's body far in the future. Willie's open mouth was half-way to a scream: he finished the job.

Immediately gentle arms enfolded him, pressing his face against the soft front of her gown. "There, there, there," crooned the warm voice. "It's all over now. We thought we'd lost you, but there's no need to worry any more."

"Isn't there?" threatened the other voice. "I think this calls for the punishment seat."

"Oh, no, dear," pleaded the voice over Willie's head. "He won't do it again."

"He certainly won't if I can help it," snapped the white-gowned man.

Willie's brain was whirling overtime. Although the two adults looked as though they were working in a hospital, they talked about this place as being home. And they treated Willie as though . . . "Are you his father and mother?" he asked.

The man, who had started to stride away, swung round again to face Willie. The woman gave a little gasp as her arm slid from Willie's shoulder.

"We're *your* father and mother, Willie, darling," she said.

"Willie? Is his name Willie, too?"

The man took a deep breath and let it out again very slowly. "He's up to something again," he muttered through clenched teeth.

53

"Oh, Willie, dear, not today," pleaded the other Willie's mother. "You've already upset us quite enough, getting tangled in Father's new machine, and lying there on your bed without moving for ever so long, and – and everything."

"I'm just beginning to understand," snapped the other Willie's father. "He wasn't unconscious at all. He was playing games with us again. Remember the time when he pretended he had lost his memory? Just because he didn't want to go to class that day. Remember the time he told the newscast that he wasn't our son at all, and that we'd found him on the doorstep? Remember when he spread the rumour that I'd blown myself up in the laboratory, and we were swamped with flowers and get-well wishes? Some jokes go too far, and he has got to learn when to stop."

Willie found himself disliking the other Willie more and more; and positively began to hate him as his father went on, "Just let him try anything else today, and he'll be in the punishment seat before his feet touch the ground." Willie had no idea what the punishment seat might be, but he was quite sure he wanted to keep out of it. If he told these people what had happened to him, would they believe him or would they assume he was indulging in another silly practical joke? He decided to postpone any revelations, at least until Father had gone off the boil.

"He can be a very good boy – sometimes," said the mother with a wan smile.

"Huh!" grunted the father figure. "Well, he's wasted enough time for us for one day. Let's have breakfast."

"Ah," thought Willie. "At least that explains why everyone is wearing night-shirts, caps and socks." Feeling that he ought to keep up his reputation for being a good boy – sometimes – he added aloud brightly, "I'll just get dressed then," only to be daunted by the looks turned on him.

"Willie," whispered his mother hastily, "you mustn't try to make jokes so early in the morning. You know it upsets your father."

Willie was quick to realise what was wrong, and did his best to put matters right. "Oh, yes," he giggled. "It was – waking up so suddenly. I forgot that I – was dressed – already."

"Well, just to show what a good boy you really can be,

He found himself in the next room

run along and set up the table for father." As Mother patted his shoulder and smiled down at him, Willie's heart sank into his bedsocks. Where was the table in this place? And how did one set it up?

The first step at least was to stand up and look as though he meant business. As he slid from whatever piece of furniture he was sitting on, it hissed like a deflating balloon, crumpled in on itself and disappeared into the floor. Indeed it seemed to be part of the floor. Willie tried not to show his bewilderment when he realised that in the smooth white walls there were no windows or doors. Which was the way from the room?

"Don't put yourself out," snapped father. He strode irritably into the middle of the nearest wall – and straight through it.

The other's mother sighed and followed him. The wall appeared to be solid, yet they had passed through it like ghosts. On the other side a voice he was quickly coming to recognise roared "Willie!" Crossing his fingers Willie walked hesitantly up to the white expanse: and found himself in the next room. He might have slipped through a very thin cloud.

Mother and father were already seated on very tall white cushions at table. The table was almost empty with a plate and beaker in front of each parent, and an object like a telephone without a receiver by father's right elbow. Both he and mother were eating with a piece of cutlery that seemed to be knife, fork and spoon in one. Willie could see neither a place set for him nor a seat, but father nodded towards one side of him, and Willie shuffled to the space indicated. As he stood undecided, mother with a sigh touched the table in front of him. Immediately a cushion rose up behind him so suddenly he lost his balance and, startled, fell on to it.

"Don't sit there all day thinking about it," grumbled father. "Dial your breakfast, and get on with it." Then, to Willie's relief, he unwittingly demonstrated, by spinning a series of numbers on the telephone-like instrument: whereupon a plateful of what appeared to be brown ping-pong balls popped up at his hand through the surface of the table. He pushed the instrument towards Willie, who chose numbers at random.

In front of him materialised a bowl full of a steaming green mess. The hiss of a sudden intake of breath near to
56

his left ear indicated that he had done the wrong thing again.

"Plankton puree for breakfast?"

"He takes after me. Sometimes I feel like eating the oddest things at most peculiar times," murmured mother distractedly. "Aren't you going to have anything with it, dear?"

"He'd better if he doesn't want to be sick," muttered father. "Go on. Dial."

Thus encouraged, Willie poked a reluctant finger at the dial, and was rewarded with another bellow from an outraged parent. "Chocolate sauce? He's going to put chocolate sauce on that seaweed slop!"

"I just wondered what it would taste like," explained Willie unconvincingly.

Father struggled valiantly to contain his temper. "You're trying to show off, that's what you are doing. You just want to be noticed."

Unfair, thought Willie, when to be noticed was the one thing he was trying to avoid. But how could he, when this world was beyond his wildest dreams?

Grimly father poked the dial and the dishes in front of Willie sank into the table again. Equally grimly father ordered a beaker full of white liquid, which he thumped down in front of Willie. "Get on with that."

Uncertainly Willie took a sip. What might these people drink? Then he smiled. "Why, it's milk," he said.

"And as soon as you've finished it, you're coming with me," rasped father, after choking on one of the brown balls.

"Oh, please," pleaded mother. "He's only a little boy. Remember what you were like at his age."

But the tears Father wiped from his eyes were caused by the crumb in his throat, and not by any tender feelings towards the boy. He pinched Willie's ear firmly between his finger and thumb, and in spite of his supposed son's squeaks and mother's wails, led the boy through another wall.

The room into which they emerged was as cluttered as the others had been bare, an odd mixture of museum and workshop. Willie was pulled rapidly past exhibits displayed in neatly-labelled cases. Trying to see as much as possible, he thought he recognised a food-mixer and a coffee-pot. At the same time, benches round the room were filled with inexplicable pieces of apparatus made of contorted tubing, dials, switches and coils of wire. From the ceiling dangled what might have been a series of hair driers similar to the one Willie's real father had bought for his real mother on her last birthday. There was little time to speculate, though, as Willie was pushed unceremoniously towards what seemed to be a dentist's chair.

"Is that the punishment seat?" asked Willie apprehensively.

"If you didn't recognise it at once, then obviously it hasn't been used enough." Father caught himself shouting again, and paused. "I don't know what game you're playing this time, but it is going to stop right now. Understand? Now."

The barked order brought another person hurrying through the wall. He was an ungainly individual in the awkward age between teenager and young man. He was dressed in the usual cap, gown and socks, but they were of rougher material and coloured green.

"You called, master?" he asked, cringing slightly as he spoke.

"Who – I? You're on duty early this morning, Green."

"Keen, master, I am." With a sidelong squint at Willie through piggy eyes. "Minister were up before us, though. Asking for you, master. Something to do with the new memory machine."

"Urgent, is it?"

"Would wish you to port over to the Ministry as soon as convenient, master."

"Right." Father turned to Willie. "You stay here. I'll deal with you when I get back." He strode through a wall, and was gone.

Green gave a giggle so malicious it made Willie shudder. "For it again, are you? What you been doing this time? No matter, it'll be a pleasure to see you squirm."

"What have I done to you?" demanded Willie.

Green held up a bandaged finger. Willie was almost reassured to see such a crude piece of first aid among so many technological marvels. "This, for instance. Somebody put one of them exhibit mousetraps where somebody else wasn't expecting it. Might have cut my finger off, it might."

"Oh, I am sorry," murmured Willie.

"Sorry? I heard you laughing three rooms away. Well, I'll hear you yelling for a change."

Willie decided the time had come to correct certain misapprehensions. "I'm not who you think I am," he said.

"Oh, you want to play another of your games."

"This isn't a game. I'm not him. I'm me."

"That's funny," sniggered the youth. "I'm me, too. But the you me is a White, Master's pride and joy; while the me me is only a Green – Assistant Underkeeper of the Winkie Museum."

"What's the Winkie Museum?"

"Master's going to love this game," chortled Green, rubbing his hands. "Worth six of the best any day."

"I tell you I don't understand. Please explain."

"Keep it up, boy. At this rate you'll earn full force." Gloatingly he smacked his lips as he indicated the chair. "It – er – transmits – feelings to whoever is sitting in it. Which, depending on the setting, vary from a gentle pat to an almighty swish with a springy cane. Whee – Ouch! Improvement on the old-fashioned whacking because it's controlled: saves energy for the walloper and can't physically damage the walloped, because it's only brainwaves. Master's a genius with brainwaves." He squinted at the chair. "Takes up too much room, though. Only really suitable for schools. We're working on a portable version, though, then every home can have one."

"It sounds awful," breathed Willie.

"You ought to know," chuckled Green. "If it wasn't for having you round the house, I doubt Master would have dreamed it up."

Now two urgent problems faced Willie. The most important was to get home; but the most pressing was to avoid a personal demonstration of the punishment seat. He decided to put as much distance as possible between himself and the fiendish contraption. He ran to the nearest wall, not caring which room he found himself in as long as it was not this one. However instead of passing through a layer of mist as before, he bounced off the wall as though it was made of rubber.

"Ho-ho," cackled Green. "I just turned the force-field up to maximum. Nobody gets in or out till Master comes back. I'm Underkeeper and I'm keeping you. Oh, aren't you going to wriggle! Set mousetraps, would you?"

"I didn't," protested Willie. "I keep trying to tell you

I'm – well – believe it or not – I'm really your Willie's great-great-great-grandfather."

Green's convulsions of laughter might almost have been a fit. "Keep it up, young 'un," he wheezed. "At this rate the punishment seat's going to blow a fuse."

Despondently Willie slumped against a display case. Why should anybody believe him?

"Sir William Winkie are you, boy? Started with that old can-opener, did you?"

Willie glanced at the object on display by his elbow. According to a diagram on the case it could at the same time open a can, deposit the contents into a saucepan or basin and reduce the container to a small cube of metal. Yet it was so simple Willie could almost work out how the gadget operated.

"You invented the better mousetrap, did you?" A roughly bandaged finger was wagged at Willie. "Have a good look round. Remember 'em all?"

To the discordant whoops of Green's jeering laughter Willie examined the exhibits. Each was of the "Why-didn't-I-think-of-that?" order. Dozens of them, because this was the Winkie Museum. Sir William's exhibits ended with an improved portable solar heating stove, but the cases went on. "Inventors run in our family," the other Willie had said. Generations of them up to the "genius with brainwaves", who was now in conference with The Minister.

"His father is working on a Time Traveller, isn't he?" Willie mentioned casually.

"Don't you know it," snarled Green, glancing up at one of the hanging hoods. "Nearly cost me my job last week – Master finding you with your head in one of them. Just caught you in time with the dial set and your finger on the switch."

Willie peered up. Yes, there was a switch on the left side and a dial on the right. A growl from Green interrupted his speculations. "You just stay away from it."

"Don't be silly," retorted Willie. "I can't get my head into it while it hangs up there."

"You know as well as I do that you've only got to pull it down to your height."

"Like this?" Willie reached up, and the hood descended smoothly until the base rested on his shoulder. With a bellow Green hurled himself at the boy, and Willie staggered back. The edge of the punishment seat caught the back of his knees, tumbling him into the very chair he was trying to avoid. As his weight activated the mechanism, plastic bands spun round his arms, legs and waist, holding him firmly. (Another Winkie had improved seat-belts.)

"Who's a clever boy, then?" Green danced a little jig, delighted with Willie's struggles. "All ready for Master now. I'm as clever as you, aren't I?"

"No," said Willie.

The dancing stopped. "Say yes."

"No."

Green's tiny eyes narrowed until they almost disappeared. "You're in the punishment seat now, you little phkumph, and nobody can get in here. Unless you say as Im Green is as clever as all the Winkies rolled into one, I'm going to switch it on full whack." He slid behind the chair. "Ready?"

Willie might only be just starting algebra, but if he couldn't devise an escape, he thought, he didn't deserve to be a Winkie. "I'll tell father," he replied coolly. "He might want to punish me, but he won't thank you for hurting me."

"But will Master believe you? The beauty of the punishment seat is there's nothing to show after. Like enough he'll believe me when I tell him you're still at your lying games. Then like enough you'll get a second dose."

"If he finds me fastened in this chair, he'll believe me. And he may be back any minute."

A confused muttering suggested that Green was arguing with himself. Should he flick the switch to administer a beating, or should he release the boy? Willie braced himself, prepared for the worst, but determined not to give the Underkeeper the satisfaction of hearing him cry.

With a clunk and a click the bands fell away. Slowly and deliberately Willie stood up. "That old chair never frightened me. That's the difference between us. I don't care. You're the only one who's frightened of it."

"Me?" The Underkeeper's cheeks flushed with temper. "I'm not scared of nothing. Definitely not a chair."

"But you daren't sit in it," challenged Willie.

"Oh, daren't I?" The enraged youth pushed Willie aside and flung himself into the seat. Plastic bands clicked into place. For a minute the boy eyed the Underkeeper, whose anger drained as his apprehension rose. "You'd better let me out now. If Master finds me like this, I'll tell him you did it. Then whack!"

"Stay there a little longer." Willie returned to the plastic hood, and examined the dial, graded in years. He turned a deaf ear to the torrent of pleas and abuse poured out behind him. Did he really only have to set the dial and flick a switch? A needle pointed to Willie's own year. Could it be that the setting had not been changed since he had been whisked from his own bed?

Another voice joined the Underkeeper's threats and accusations. Father, returning in a hurry, had just bounced off the wall outside. With the force-field at maximum, nobody could get in. Was Father thumping the wall, or could Willie hear his own heart beating?

With his head inside the hood Willie could see nothing – until, after flicking the switch, a few seconds of familiar fireflies. Then he opened his eyes on the stars through his bedroom window.

"About time, too," said another angry voice inside his head. "Leaving me here."

"I hope next time your father tries to fetch you back, he collects the right one of us," thought Willie. "And – do me a favour – don't play with the Time Traveller again."

"Don't worry," retorted the other Willie. "I don't want to be stuck in your rotten time. Call this a bed?"

"Funny sort of walls you have," mused Willie.

"Force-fields," corrected the other condescendingly. "They can be put up – just like that – wherever you like. My grandfather invented them."

"Suppose a force-field was turned to maximum: could a person ever get through?" asked Willie apprehensively.

"Only by turning off the power at the central point. But nobody would ever be so stupid, because then *all* the walls would disappear." Then the superior attitude crumpled with a mental gasp. "You didn't . . ."

"I didn't," agreed Willie. "But you're going to be blamed for it."

"Well, of all the mean, deceitful, underhand . . ." The second voice abruptly faded. Presumably father had at last got in. Willie was suddenly alone again.

He stretched his legs. What bliss it was to be in his own bed and pyjamas again. He realised that he was tired. Drowsy memories hovered around the edges of sleep. He knew that he hadn't been dreaming, but in the light of morning he might not be so sure. Sir William Winkie, the celebrated inventor! Did that really lie in the future? He tried to picture that can-opener. Could he remember how it worked? He must try. In the middle of trying, he fell asleep.

THE INVASION

by ROGER MALISSON

Mick Carter heard the assembly bell ring when he was on the top of Hannock Hill.

It made a sweet, tinny sound on the early morning air and would have been quite pleasant to hear if only Mick had been listening to it down in the School Hall and not on Hannock Hill, because then he would have been on time for school for once. Whereas now he was going to be late as usual. He glanced at his watch and groaned. No, *later* than usual. It would take him a good twenty minutes to get down the lane, through Hannock Woods and out on to the main street of Hannock Village, even if he ran. He started running.

The reasons for Mick's continual lateness were no less a puzzle to himself than to his teachers. It wasn't as if he disliked school particularly – it was just that he had an extraordinary amount of difficulty in parting from his bed in the mornings. No matter how he rushed and scrambled, he was very rarely in the assembly hall before the arrival, at nine o'clock sharp, of the headmaster. It was, Mick had decided, just one of those things he was stuck with and had to make the best of.

As he sped down the hill and into the woods he sorted through all the excuses he could make. He always thought of a good excuse when he was late, the more elaborate the better, and it did not worry him especially that he was never believed. All the other boys in class looked to him to come up with a good story, like the time he had said he was late because his mother had won the pools and fainted when she had opened the letter.

"I couldn't just leave her stretched out on the lino, sir, could I?" he'd wound up appealingly.

That had been a good one; and so had the story about the bank robbery in the High Street. For half a minute there he'd had old Polly Perkins, their form master, wavering in belief. (Mick had been the one to think up Mr. Perkin's nickname, inspired by the shape of his large hooked nose.)

Mick slowed up as he ran round the corner into Hannock Woods. He had a stitch in his side and anyway the lane was pot-holed in places. He jumped a couple of puddles, lost his gym kit in one, fished it out and jogged on again, deep into the woods. The tall trees were all around, cutting him off from the village and the farms nearby, although he could hear the distant sounds of traffic in the High Street and the noise of a tractor ploughing.

Panting heavily, he rounded a curve in the lane and then stopped dead. Blocking the lane was a circular metal disc, about fifteen feet high and thirty wide. It had crushed the earth of the banked lane on either side, and crumbled dirt and weeds lay on the gleaming metal surface. A starling was perched on the top, but it flew off as Mick approached. Nothing else showed any sign of life.

Mick shouted loudly for someone to come, banged his knuckles on the curved side of the disc and kicked it a couple of times, but no-one replied. He drew back and stared at the thing with annoyance. He had no idea what it was. He knew what it looked like – a flying saucer – but Mick was not interested in space and as far as he was concerned it was just a heap of junk blocking his way.

It was going to make him *really* late. Muttering rude things to himself he started to climb up the sides of the disc where he could get a foothold in the soft, broken earth of the bank. He scrambled madly for a moment at the smooth metal and with a grunt hauled himself on to the top. The surface below his feet felt slightly warm, even through the soles of his shoes.

Mick glanced quickly round and was about to start down the other side when the metal top suddenly gave way and he plunged down into the darkness inside the disc.

He landed on something soft and rubbery which cushioned his fall nicely, and he lay there recovering for a moment. Then the softness beneath him began slowly to wriggle away. Mick got up hastily and rubbed his eyes.

It was not completely dark. A reddish glow shone from

the walls and gave enough light for Mick to see the unfortunate creature he had landed on, which was now standing by the wall. It was rather like a large octopus and it was making threatening gestures with its tentacles. Mick stared at it in disbelief and the creature stared back.

"Do not be afraid, Earthling," it said at last in a quavery voice that came out of a box like a radio slung across its body. Its tentacles waxed excitedly.

Mick was too surprised and curious to feel any fear.

"I'm not afraid," he said, standing up.

"Do not be afr – ah. Very well. Very well. Yes, good." The creature seemed a little confused and not sure what to say next. There was a short pause. "No doubt you are wondering where you are," it ventured at last.

"I know where I am," said Mick calmly. "Hannock Woods."

"Hannock Woods," the creature repeated heavily. It whirled round, stubbed a tentacle at a button on a desk, and immediately a whole section of the wall lit up brightly. An image of the Earth appeared on it, as seen from space, then a close-up picture of the African continent, then an even closer picture of the jungles and rivers. The creature

"You're on the wrong continent."

played with a knob and the picture changed wildly, swinging from jungle to desert.

Mick watched patiently and finally said, "If you're looking for Hannock Woods on your map you're on the wrong continent. We're in Europe. England. Eighty-three miles from London."

"London!" yelped the creature excitedly, and twiddled the knob. A picture of Nelson's Column came up, with pigeons flying around it.

"Due north of London," added Mick helpfully.

The creature paused, muttering Eighty-three – divide by nine, multiply by 7.35 . . ." Evidently it was trying to convert from miles into its own scale of distance. The struggle was nearly too much for it. At one point Mick noticed it surreptitiously counting on its tentacles. Eventually, however, it adjusted the knob and a picture of Hannock Woods came up on the screen. Slap in the middle of it was the gleaming metal disc. The creature gave a cry of joy. It pushed another button and another patch of wall, a smaller one, lit up. Tiny symbols were shining on it. Mick guessed they were figures and the creature had somehow got its bearings from them. Presumably it now knew where it was.

"So," said the creature in a confident voice as it turned round again to face him, "you have been of assistance, Earthling. Rest assured I shall bear it in mind when the invasion is accomplished."

Invasion? A tremor of doubt went through Mick's mind. It took a lot to divert his attention from his personal problems (in this case being late for school five days in a row) to possible dangers for humanity, but the word 'invasion' did it. Was this creature really serious?

"What invasion?" he asked cautiously.

The creature bounced excitedly on four of its legs.

"We of the glorious Vedan Imperial Space Fleet are about to annex your planet, Earthling," it said pompously, and then went on quickly, "In fact it has already been annexed. Since I landed I have played our Imperial Anthem and announced the formal subjugation of your world to the will of the Imperial Authority." It stopped for a moment and then added kindly, "Congratulations."

"You mean you've conquered us?" asked Mick incredulously, sinking on to a chair-like pedestal fixed to the floor. "All by yourself?"

"It is not a question of conquest," answered the creature. "We are a civilised race. If we have annexed you, it is entirely for your own benefit. Force will not be necessary either. A mere demonstration of our power will be sufficient to make any Earthling conscious of the futility of resistance. When the skies of London, the capital city of Africa, are filled by the mighty spectacle of the Vedan Fleet – "

"London's not the capital of Africa," Mick broke in. He was bad at geography but he was fairly sure of that. "London isn't even *in* Africa."

The octopus-creature threshed its tentacles in annoyance, and went on impatiently, "When the armed forces of the Planet Veda land upon the Chinese Coast, and the Atlantic Seas around it are covered by the invincible army of Veda – "

"Who says China's got an Atlantic Coast?" Mick interrupted again. "It's by the Pacific Ocean. Didn't they teach you Earth geography before you came?"

The creature emitted a series of shrill beeps and its brownish-mottled skin turned purple. Mick recognised the signs of temper from the times when he had contradicted Mr. Perkins. These creatures, like teachers, did not like to be told they were in the wrong.

"All right," he said hastily. "It doesn't matter. If you want to think China's in the Atlantic, go ahead."

The creature puffed itself up; an alarming sight.

"I myself," it said coldly, "have surveyed this planet, mapped it, and monitored your Earth's broadcasts so thoroughly that I even know your ridiculous local names for the different parts of your world – New York, Old York, Paris, Wigan and Kong Hong."

"Hong Kong, you mean," muttered Mick automatically, but the creature did not hear. It continued to reel off a jumbled list of place names, meanwhile giving Mick time to think. Evidently this Vedan, or whatever it called itself, was acting as a kind of scout for some alien spacefleet. Its job must be to find planets suitable for invasion, check them over and then whistle up the big guns to finish the task. Nor, as he looked around him, could Mick doubt that the Vedan Imperial whatsit must be quite a force to be reckoned with. Even though the Vedan was not especially impressive in itself, the ship it was flying was obviously built by a civilisation far more advanced than Earth's.

This was serious. It might even mean a war. Mick thought fast. There was no point in making it angry, because that wouldn't solve anything. But somehow he had to put the creature off the idea of trying to take over the earth. That was it – he had to stop it *wanting* to annex the world. Mick drew a deep breath. It was a very slim chance.

"Rome, Timbuctoo and Batterseafunfair," the creature wound up breathlessly, with a final triumphant wave of its tentacles. "See? I know your Earth very well, my friend."

"Yes, you do indeed," Mick agreed politely. "And when you annex Earth, are you going to annex the Sea as well?" he leaned forward with a meaningful stare and lowered his voice. "Or are you leaving . . . *them* alone?"

"Sea? Sea?" The creature plaited its front tentacles in confusion. "How do you mean, Sea?"

"I mean the people under the Sea," Mick went on blandly. "What are you going to do about . . . *them*?"

"Yes – yes – the people *under* the Sea; of course. Yes, well, we shall annex them too." The creature played cat's-cradle with its tentacles for a moment, and suddenly burst out, "How many of them are there, would you say? People under the Sea?"

"Two hundred and ninety-eight million, give or take a few hundred thousand," said Mick promptly. "At the last count . . . but you know how it is, you can't keep up with them can you? They breed like tadpoles down there."

"Quite. Quite so," agreed the creature. Its skin was changing colour again from purple to blue.

"Anyhow, we don't have much to do with them up here," Mick said, improvising for all he was worth. This Vedan was even more of a sucker than Polly Perkins! "You know why, of course."

"Of course," agreed the alien instantly. Then it said sharply, "Why?"

"Well, you know." Mick shrugged. "They're just generally – pretty disgusting. So violent! Always looking for trouble! There was a time you hardly dared take a boat out for a sail for fear of them attacking."

"But I have often observed," argued the alien in a puzzled voice, "That sometimes at special cities along your coasts such as Blackpool and Sunnybrighton, the inhabitants remove most of their clothes and rush into the waves – why do they do this? I have never understood it. And if the people under the Sea are so violent, why are your people not afraid to do it?"

"Sacrifices," said Mick in a tragic voice, shaking his head. "That's how we keep the peace with them – the people under the Sea. You've seen herds of our people rushing *into* the Sea – have you ever counted how many come *out*?"

"Dreadful!" the creature exclaimed, greatly shocked.

"What a comfort for us now we're under Vedan protection, though," Mick went on, relaxing happily. "You'll sort them out for us, won't you?"

"All two hundred and fifty-eight million," the Vedan murmured faintly to itself.

"Two hundred and ninety-eight," Mick corrected it cheerfully.

"Thank you. Two hundred and ninety-eight."

There was an awkward silence.

"It's very brave really," Mick said admiringly. "I mean, considering."

"Considering what?"

"Considering that the favourite food of the people under the Sea is . . ." Mick paused for effect.

"What *is* it?" the creature finally asked, with something like a frightened giggle.

"Octopus," smiled Mick.

The Vedan shot out a tentacle and punched a button in the wall. A noise like saucepans being mended immediately filled the air and the alien stiffened into a kind of salute, waited for the 'music' to stop and then rattled off an announcement in its own language.

"What are you doing?" asked Mick as he jumped to his feet, although he had already, gleefully, guessed.

"I have played the Imperial Anthem and formally liberated this planet. You are no longer a part of the Vedan Empire. You are insufficiently civilised to be worthy of the honour," the creature gabbled. "Kindly leave. I shall be taking off soon." It hurriedly clicked a switch and a slot appeared in the wall through which Mick could see the green of Hannock Woods, comfortingly familiar.

"It's not fair," said Mick resentfully, getting ready to leave.

"I know. I'm sorry. Please hurry," the alien said. It more or less pushed Mick outside into the lane, waved a farewell tentacle and suddenly disappeared as the door slot closed over. Mick ran for cover and was only just in time to throw himself down behind the bank of the lane when the ground shook, the metal disc trembled, rotated, rose and, with a great tearing noise that set Mick's teeth on edge, vanished in a twinkling into the blue sky. There was a second's silence and then the birdsong came back, Mick could hear the sound of a tractor in the distance and nothing was left to show that a spaceship had even been there except for two dents in the banks either side of Hannock Lane.

Mick turned to go and as he did, he realised with a start that he was going to be later than ever. He glanced at his watch.

Quarter to ten!

With a whoop Mick went running off down the lane into the village and along the street to the school gates. It was only as he dashed through them that he realised he had not thought of a good story to explain why he was late, and decided that he had better tell the truth for once.

His classmates agreed afterwards that Mick had excelled himself that morning. It might have got him five days' detention, but surely it was worth it to see the look on Polly Perkins' face when he heard Mick Carter explain that he was late for school because he had been persuading an octopus in a spaceship that it ought not to invade Earth...

THE TOYS OF EARTH

by Pamela Cleaver

In November it begins to get dark at about four o'clock so Tom and Angela Fisher, coming home across the moors in the school bus, could not be really sure that their eyes had not deceived them. After the bus had dropped them off at the end of the lane leading to their farm, they talked about it.

"What do you think it was then?" said Tom. "That thing in Hobb's Spinney?"

"It looked like one of the UFOs they're always writing about in the Sunday papers," said his sister, "but then it seemed too big for that."

"That's what I thought it looked like," said Tom. "But it couldn't have been. We must have imagined it – flying saucers and little green men just don't exist."

"Well, shall we go and look?" suggested Angela.

Tom thought about it. "No," he said. "It's half a mile back, and it's nearly dark and I want my tea."

"All right," said Angela. "Tomorrow's Saturday. No school, so we can go and look in the morning. If there really was something there, I daresay it'll still be there then."

So they trudged home to Markyate Farm, their waiting tea and their homework.

Next morning, Mr. Fisher was out early as usual, milking the cows, and when the children came down to breakfast they heard him saying to their mother, "Billy Barcombe had his tractor stolen last night."

"Well I never," said Mrs. Fisher. "Do they know who took it?"

"Mick says the Barcombes heard noises, but they didn't think much about it at the time – Charley Fox after hens, they guessed."

Mrs. Fisher was spooning egg into little Sam's mouth. Sam was sitting in his highchair, his mouth opening as the spoon came towards him, reminding Angela of a baby bird in its nest.

"Burglars are pretty rare in these parts, aren't they Dad?" Tom asked.

"Folks round here haven't much worth stealing," sniffed Mr. Fisher. "Who'd have thought anyone would want a broken-down old tractor like Billy's? He was going to buy a new one next week anyway."

Tom and Angela ate their breakfast, helped their mother with the dishes while Sam was put in his playpen with some toys, and then they put on their gumboots and anoraks and went out.

"Hobb's Spinney?" said Angela.

"Right," said Tom, and they moved off across the moorland which ran right up to their farmyard gate. They trudged over the coarse tussocks of grass and wiry heather that clothed the ground, down into the valley, avoiding the patches of bog. They jumped over the stream and puffed up the steep hill beyond. At the top the ground began to slope gently towards a clump of trees known as Hobb's Spinney.

"I can see a sort of silvery glint," said Angela. "I do believe there *is* something there."

"Well, let's not rush at it," said Tom. "We'll creep round and have a quiet sort of look."

Angela nodded and they began to move stealthily the way they did when they were pretending to be Indians on the prairie. Approaching like that, they did not see what was there until they were almost upon it and when they did, it stopped them in their tracks. It was an enormous silvery object shaped like a huge humming top.

"It's as big as the farmhouse, the barn and the milking parlour all put together!" said Angela.

"And look there!" breathed Tom, pointing. "Billy Barcombe's tractor!"

"*And* Mr. Forrest's bicycle and the butcher's van!" said Angela. And that was not all. The area round the shining object was like a totter's yard – there were pillar boxes, gates, telephone kiosks, cars, bikes, vans and tractors, all jumbled together.

"How on earth did they get here?" Angela wanted to know.

"I've no idea," said Tom. "But I don't like it. There's something sinister going on. I'm going home . . ."

At that moment, a door slid open in the side of the humming top and to the children's amazement and disbelief a person stepped out who must have been at least six metres tall. He had long silvery hair and was dressed in a close-fitting purplish garment. He was like a man in every respect except for his size.

"It's a giant," whispered Angela in an awed voice. "He's three times as big as Dad!"

"That's who took Billy Barcombe's tractor," said Tom. "And all those other things."

"But what for?" asked Angela.

"Keep still!" hissed Tom. "Wait until his back's turned and then we'll leg it as fast as we can for the village."

The giant seemed to be a quiet and peaceful person. His face was not at all frightening but there was a curious foreignness about it that made the children wonder where he

"He's got Billy Barcombe's tractor . . . and the butcher's van!"

came from. He did not seem at all a *fee fi fo fum* sort of giant, nevertheless, the children were not anxious to be spotted. When he took a huge stride away from his hum-

73

ming top and bent down to examine his collection, the children wriggled back the way they had come and then ran for it.

When they thought they were well out of earshot they stopped to draw breath.

"What are we going to do?" asked Angela.

"We're going to the village to tell Police Constable Forrest where his bicycle and all the other stolen objects are. We'll warn him about the giant, but don't be surprised if he doesn't believe us."

"But it's true."

"Yes, but you know what grown ups are like – they won't believe children who talk about giants and such."

"Well, they'll have to when they see him, won't they?" said Angela indignantly. "Seeing is believing."

"You wait and see if I'm not right," said Tom darkly.

"Where do you think he came from and why do you think he took all those things?" Angela asked as they got near the village.

"I reckon he's an alien from another planet," said Tom, "and that that thing like a humming top is his space ship. I reckon he's on an exploratory mission and he's come here to see what our world is like and that he's collecting all that stuff as samples of the kind of things to be found on earth."

"Gosh," said Angela, impressed. "Do you mean he's going to take them away with him?"

"Probably. And what's more," said Tom grimly, "he may want specimens of people too, so whoever goes out to see him had better be jolly careful."

It all worked out just as Tom had predicted. P.C. Forrest admitted that he had lost his bike, that there had been several vehicles stolen in the night as well as a pillar box and a telephone kiosk mysteriously uprooted. He was amazed but delighted when Tom told him the whole lot could be found in Hobb's Spinney but he became quite angry when Tom added that they had been stolen by a giant in a huge flying saucer. He was very surprised that young Angela Fisher burst into tears when he scoffed with disbelief.

"There, there," he said. "I didn't mean to hurt your feelings." And he quickly revised his ideas and decided the thief was probably an exceptionally tall man in some new-fangled kind of foreign car. Being a cautious man, he decided not to take chances, so got on to the nearest town by phone to ask for reinforcements to help him deal with a daring thief who might be dangerous.

"Can we come too and watch from a distance?" Tom wanted to know.

P.C. Forrest hrrrmphed and said heavily they'd best be getting home but that he would let them know how it turned out.

At lunchtime the telephone rang and when Mr. Fisher came back to the table after answering it, his expression was grim.

"What have you two been up to?" he asked. "That was Mr. Forrest – he's bringing a Chief Superintendent from Taunton over to talk to you both."

"It's all right, Dad," Tom said. "Angela and I found Billy Barcombe's stolen tractor and a whole lot of other stuff. I expect he's coming to thank us."

"Well I never!" said Mrs. Fisher.

"Twactor!" shouted Sam joyfully, banging the toy tractor he was holding in his hand on to the tray of his high chair while opening his mouth wide for another spoonful of sieved carrot.

Tom was only partly right about Chief Superintendent Andrews wanting to thank them. He did, but he also wanted a detailed statement about exactly how they had come upon the humming top and how the giant had behaved. Mr. Forrest apologised for not believing them when they had told him about the giant. Tom, encouraged by the Chief Super's manner, told him his theory about the giant being from another world and collecting the various things as examples of earth's hardware.

"Yes, we think that too," said Andrews, "but I don't think he's after people. He didn't touch the police car while we were inside it, but when we got out, he took that and added it to his collection. We've tried talking to him, but of course he doesn't understand our language. He speaks to us, but we don't know what he's saying."

"Can you not communicate at all?" asked Mr. Fisher.

"No, we've tried sign language, but he doesn't seem very intelligent – at least not in our ways. He must be, of course, as he's a member of a race that has discovered space travel. We've sent for the military and for someone from the Space Agency to bring a CETI, but that'll take time."

"What's a CETI?" Angela asked.

"It's a special computer for translating communications from extra-terrestrial intelligences," said Andrews. "It runs sounds through, analyses them and compares them with all the other sounds so far discovered during space travel."

"What's going to happen meanwhile?" Tom asked.

"The army are moving in to guard the area," Andrews told them. "We're grateful to you children for finding this for us and reporting it to Mr. Forrest, which is just what you should have done, but we must warn you to keep clear of the area from now on. We'll let you know what happens."

"You're not going to shoot him, are you?" Angela asked anxiously. "He seemed quite gentle."

"Certainly not," said Andrews. "At least not unless he turns violent. We don't want to start an international – I mean intergalactic – incident."

The two policemen got up to go. "There's just one thing more," said the Chief Super. "We want to keep this situation as quiet as we can – the fewer people who know about it the better. We don't want sightseers complicating the issue, so don't talk to anyone about it, and if any journalists come snooping around, don't tell them anything, O.K.?"

Tom and Angela agreed not to talk about it, but they had no intention of staying tamely at home and pretending the whole thing had never happened. It was the most exciting thing in their lives so far. They slipped out of the house soon after the policemen left, taking Tom's telescope with them, and before long were ensconced in a vantage point where they could see everything that was happening without being seen.

The army had thrown a cordon round Hobb's Spinney, a barrier of barbed wire and armed soldiers, some army lorries and tanks at strategic intervals round the perimeter.

"I think that's silly," said Angela. "If he wanted to, he could step over the wire, pick up the tanks and add them to his collection." She was staring through the telescope.

"What's he doing?" Tom wanted to know. "Come on, it's my turn with the telescope."

"Just a minute," said Angela, "I haven't had my five minutes yet. He's sitting down, moving the cars and things about. Do you know what it reminds me of, Tom? He looks just like Sam when he sits in his playpen and has a game with his little cars."

Tom snatched the telescope. "Yes," he said, "it does look just like that. One of the soldiers is going towards him, calling through a megaphone . . . Hey – it *is* like Sam! The giant has put his arm round the cars to shield them from the officer and is shouting back . . . Just like Sam when I want to look at something of his and he shouts, 'Go 'way – mine!' . . . Do you know what he's doing now? he's picked up the man, quite gently, and put him back on the other side of the wire. Hey, what's that noise?"

Even though they had not heard any of the shouted conversation between the man and the giant, the noise that was filling the air was easily audible to them. It must have been deafening in Hobb's Spinney because the soldiers all had their hands over their ears. It was a very high-pitched staccato buzzing like a huge, angry bee. The giant looked up and listened. Tom focussed the telescope on the giant's face. The alien's expression was half fearful, half defiant.

"He looks like Sam when he's had a ticking off," said Tom.

The giant got up, went to his humming top and brought out a box. He began to activate it in some way and the same sort of angry bee noises came from it. "That was a signal," said Angela. "He's sending a reply. Now perhaps we shall see some action. I wonder if it's from other people like him wanting to know whether to land?"

"Maybe," said Tom. "But I don't think so. He looks cross and he's going back to the humming top . . . he's taking Billy Barcombe's tractor with him."

"Do let me look," said Angela, snatching the telescope.

The air was filled again with angry buzzing. She saw the look on the giant's face. He opened his mouth and gave a roar of anger which the children could hear even from their safe distance. The buzzing persisted and the giant sulkily hurled the tractor away from him, narrowly missing a tank just outside the wire. He got inside the humming top and while the children watched, the huge silvery craft lifted straight up into the air with incredible speed and soon was no more than a silver dot in the sky. There was another burst of the staccato signalling and then everything was quiet again.

For half an hour nothing happened. They scanned the sky but the silver dot had gone and showed no signs of reappearing. Another half an hour passed and Tom and Angela decided it was all over.

"Besides," said Tom, "the soldiers must think so too; they're beginning to pack up."

It was hard to return to the ordinary life of the farm and going to school after such an exciting incident. The children visited Hobb's Spinney several times during the following week but the humming top did not come back. Gradually all the stolen vehicles were returned to their owners – except for Billy Barcombe's tractor which had been smashed when the giant threw it, but that didn't matter because he had had a new one on order and it arrived the following Wednesday.

Tom and Angela were dying to tell their friends what had happened but they kept the secret as Chief Superintendent Andrews had asked them to; anyway, they decided it would be a pretty tall tale to ask anyone to swallow who had not seen the evidence with their own eyes.

On Friday afternoon, exactly a week after they had first sighted the strange thing in Hobb's Spinney, they got home from school to be greeted by their mother, who said, "You've got a visitor. Go into the sitting room and I'll bring your tea in there."

Chief Superintendent Andrews was waiting for them. "I thought you would like to know the end of the story," he said. And while they ate their scones and jam, he told them.

"The CETI arrived too late for us to make contact with the alien, but everything he had said had been recorded on tape and also some messages which came to him from space, along with his replies. When the CETI had done its work, we were amazed at what we'd learned." The police officer smiled.

"That alien, whom we had all assumed was a fully grown being because of his size, was just a child of his race. He had apparently taken a space-craft without his parent's knowledge and was out on the spree. He had landed on earth just to collect some new toys, which is what our vehicles were to him. The message he got was from his father saying in effect, 'come home at once, you naughty boy!' He had an argument with his old man but agreed to go home. He tried to sneak a tractor into his space craft with him, but somehow his father could see what he was doing and told him to put it back, that he was to take nothing with him away from earth – that was how the tractor got smashed; he was furious at not being able to keep his new toy. What do you think of that?"

"We guessed!" said Angela laughing.

"You what?" said Andrews in astonishment.

"We guessed," said Tom. "You see, we couldn't resist watching so we were hidden away safely and saw the whole thing. The way he was behaving with the cars and so on was just like our baby brother Sam when we try to take his toys from him. We guessed that although he was a giant compared with us, he was just a child where he came from."

"Well," said Andrews, "you really are amazing children. We certainly had no idea until we got the messages translated. The last message of all, by the way, was an apology from our visitor's father. He said he would see his son never came back to earth to bother us again."

"It's a pity really," said Angela. "If we had had the CETI here in time we could have understood him and we could have played with him. I can think of marvellous games we could have played with a giant."

"Hmm," said the Chief Super. "That's as maybe. You might have enjoyed it but I think perhaps you're better off playing with people your own size."

Tom and Angela nodded, but they did not really agree.

PROJECT 9

by CATHERINE GLEASON

"Wake up, Mike," said Mrs. Nichols cheerfully, drawing back the curtains.

Mike sat up and blinked drowsily as the autumn sunlight flooded into his bedroom. He rubbed his eyes and yawned. There was something different about today – what was it?

"First day back at school," his Mum reminded him. "So you'll have to get up this minute, and no turning over for another five minutes' doze. I'm going to get your breakfast ready now."

"O.K., Mum." Mike struggled out of bed to get washed and dressed. The summer holiday seemed to have flown by this year, what with his two weeks in Margate, his visit to Auntie Jane's house in the country, and the long sunny days he'd spent playing with Jimmy and his other friends who lived nearby.

Well, at least I'll have a lot to say in my essay for Miss Brown, Mike thought, fumbling with the knot in his school tie. Part of the first week's homework was usually an essay that the English teacher set on 'How I spent My Holiday'.

Maybe going back to school wouldn't be too bad after all. Mike cheered up as he clattered downstairs. There was always Mr. Prendergast's lessons to look forward to, and he might even be in Mr. Prendergast's class this year, which would be fun. Old Prenny had a way of acting out his lessons that made them seem funny and exciting, and he was never too busy to help with other things too. One afternoon last term he had shown Mike how to mend his bike when the front wheel started wobbling and the chain fell off, which saved Mike a long trudge home. He thought Mr. Prendergast was the best teacher in the school.

There was a delicious smell of frying bacon in the kitchen.

" 'Morning, Mike," said his father, folding up the newspaper. Baby Susan gurgled and waved her spoon at him from her high chair. His mother set a steaming plate of bacon and eggs in front of him.

" 'Morning," said Mike. "Dad, do you think I'll be in Mr. Prendergast's class this year."

"I hope so," said his father. "He taught me when I was your age. Well – I must be off. Have a good day at school, son."

Soon after his father left for work, Mike finished his breakfast and rode off to school on his bike. He arrived in good time for assembly, and joined the crowd in the main hall with his friend Jimmy. Mr. Jenkins, the headmaster, a tall stern man, read out the list of classes for the new term. Mike nudged Jimmy in delight when he announced that they were both to be in Mr. Prendergast's class.

After assembly they charged down to their new form room, and bagged a pair of desks near the front. There was plenty of giggling, scuffling and shouting as the thirty-odd excited kids claimed their desks and settled in. The noise only died down when Mr. Prendergast walked in.

He took his place at his desk in front of the blackboard and smiled round at them all.

"Good morning, Form II. I hope you all enjoyed your holidays. Let's take the register now, shall we?"

They answered the roll-call in alphabetical order, and as they did so Mr. Prendergast looked keenly at the face of each child as he or she spoke.

"Jimmy Nedwell."

"Present."

"Michael Nichols."

"Present."

Mr. Prendergast's glance swept over him, and it was then that Mike had a terrible shock; for somehow the teacher had changed completely.

Mike sat quite still, unable to believe his eyes, while Mr. Prendergast shut the register and screwed the top back on his fountain-pen.

"Right all present and correct. Now then, let me tell you something about what we'll be doing this term . . ."

The teacher talked on, and Mike gazed at his face without hearing a word. For although this man looked like Mr. Prendergast – the same slight stoop, the same kind, lined face topped with its thick bush of grey hair, the same rather baggy grey suit as always – the manner and the personality

He wasn't the Mr. Prendergast they knew

of Mr. Prendergast was quite different. He was calmer, and didn't smile or joke so much. His eyes were distant and watchful. He didn't tug at his tie or thrust his hands into his pockets in the way that Mr. Prendergast did. In fact, Mike thought with a chill of unease, he wasn't like the teacher they knew, at all.

And the strange thing was, that nobody else seemed to have noticed.

"Don't you think there's something odd about Mr. Prendergast?" he asked Jimmy at lunchtime.

"Odd? No, I don't think so," said Jimmy in surprise. "How do you mean?"

Mike found it difficult to explain. "He just seems different from how he used to be, as if he's become . . . another person, almost."

Jimmy had a simple explanation. "You're crackers," he grinned. "There's nothing wrong with old Prenny. Come on, let's play football."

Mike wasn't satisfied. That afternoon he watched Mr. Prendergast closely for more signs of strangeness. The teacher seemed to be acting normally, but Mike noticed one or two things that aroused his suspicions further. For instance, Mr. Prendergast appeared to have some difficulty in writing on the blackboard. The first time he picked up the chalk he examined it carefully, almost as if he wasn't quite sure which end to use. And then his writing was not as Mike remembered. He always used to scribble on the board, but now he printed, very slowly and painstakingly, and some of his letters were oddly-shaped. In fact, Jill Jones, who was generally the first in the class to complain about anything, leaped to her feet at once.

"Please, sir, I can't read that sentence!" she called, and some of the others murmured agreement.

This seemed to upset Mr. Prendergast, who gazed at the board with a puzzled frown, as if he were trying very hard to remember something. Then he snapped his fingers, cried "Ah!" and rubbed out the words, writing them again in a way that was more like his old style.

There's something funny going on here, thought Mike.

He mentioned the odd handwriting to Jimmy after school, but his friend only laughed at him.

"It's probably just that he's out of practice after the holiday," Jimmy said. "Anyway, he's all right, old Prenny — better than most of the teachers we've got. I like him."

"Oh, I like him too," said Mike. "That's why I feel so—" he was going to say, "worried", but he didn't finish because at that moment Jimmy's bus rounded the corner and he had to run to catch it.

"See you tomorrow!" Jimmy shouted. Mike nodded, and went to fetch his bike.

On his way to the bicycle shed he saw Mr. Prendergast crossing the yard to his old Morris car which was parked near the gates. He even *walks* differently, Mike thought uneasily. Something peculiar was happening, and Mike was very curious.

"How did you get on at school today, Mike?" his Mum asked him when the family were gathered round the table for supper.

"Oh – O.K., I suppose," said Mike. "I'm in Mr. Prendergast's class."

"That's good," said his Dad, helping himself to more potatoes. "I expect you're very pleased?"

"Ye-es," said Mike slowly. "It's just that . . ."

"Well?" prompted his mother.

Mike hesitated, and then blurted out everything in a rush. "Mr. Prendergast is *different*," he said. "His writing's not the same – he doesn't seem to be able to remember things – there's something funny about him!"

His parents exchanged glances across the table, and then his father smiled.

"Mr. Prendergast is getting on you know, Mike," he said. "He must be nearly sixty now."

"That's right, dear," said Mrs. Nichols. "People do change as they get older. You just have to make allowances for them."

Mike bit his lip and said no more. They didn't understand – but then, why should they? He himself hardly understood what was going on.

But there was one thing for sure; he was going to watch Mr. Prendergast like a hawk until he found out.

The next day Mr. Prendergast took a science lesson. Form II crowded round to watch him heating blue crystals in a bell jar over a bunsen burner. They hadn't done much chemistry before, and were very surprised when their teacher, who usually took the lesson extremely slowly when he was showing them something new, suddenly began to rattle on in an alarming manner about the Second Law of Thermodynamics. There was an immediate outcry.

"We haven't done any of this before, Mr. Prendergast!"

"We don't know what you're talking about!"

"We've never heard of Thermowhatsitsname!"

"I have," declared Jill Jones, who was something of a know-it-all. "It's to do with aeroplanes, isn't it, sir?"

"No, no, that's *aero*dynamics, Mary," said Mr. Prendergast, looking dazed.

"I'm Jill, Mr. Prendergast," said Jill sounding hurt.

"That's right – sorry, Jill. And good heavens, of course you haven't heard of thermodynamics; I got carried away . . . for a moment there I thought I was . . it seemed . . ."

There was an anxious pause while Mr. Prendergast gathered his thoughts.

"Shall I get you a glass of water, sir?" offered Jimmy helpfully.

"No, I'm perfectly all right," said Mr. Prendergast rather snappishly. "We must get on with the lesson. As I was saying earlier . . ."

The class settled down, and the incident was soon forgotten by the children – with one exception. When school was over for the day, Mike waited at the bicycle shed until Mr. Prendergast left the building.

"Mr. Prendergast, may I see you for a minute?"

The teacher turned in surprise. "Why certainly, er-er . . ."

"Mike Nichols, sir."

"Of course, Mike," said Mr. Prendergast. "What can I do for you?"

"Just thought you'd like to see how well my bike's been running, sir, after you fixed it last term."

Mr. Prendergast looked blank.

"You do remember, sir?" Mike asked carefully. "You mended the chain when it broke?"

The teacher seemed to recollect. "Ah yes, the chain. The front wheel was wobbling too, wasn't it? Well, let's see it."

He led the way into the gloom of the shed and bent over the bicycle. Mike, watching him closely, suddenly noticed something weird and terrible. For the man's hair had an unnatural green tinge, and his eyes, which always used to be blue, had changed to a tawny colour, yellowish like a leopard's . . .

Mike shrank back against the door of the shed, his heart hammering with shock, unable to move. Mr. Prendergast tinkered with the bike, then raised his head.

"Yes, that seems to be all right now – "

84

He caught Mike's terrified gaze and licked his lips nervously. "Is something wrong?"

Mike tried to speak, but his voice failed him. He shook his head violently.

"Then why are you staring at me, boy?" Mr. Prendergast asked softly.

"I – it's just – I have to go now," Mike stammered.

After a moment that seemed like an hour, Mr. Prendergast shrugged and pushed the bike towards him. The dim light gleamed eerily on the pale green hair.

"Well, I shan't keep you," he said.

Mike grabbed his bike, gabbled something about being late home for tea, and almost ran out of the shed. He pedalled home as if the devil were after him, his thoughts in a turmoil.

"Mum! Mum, where are you? Come quickly!" He raced into the house, flinging his satchel on to a chair.

"Why, whatever's happened? What's all the fuss about?" cried his mother.

Mike sank on to the sofa, panting. "It's Mr. Prendergast," he gasped, when he had enough breath to speak. "He's got yellow eyes!"

"Yellow eyes . . . ?" His mother nearly dropped the teapot she was holding. "What are you talking about, Mike?"

"And green hair. I told you there was something funny about him – well, Mum – that's not Mr. Prendergast at all. *He's another person!*"

"Another person!" Mrs. Nichols repeated in amazement. "Green eyes? For goodness' sake, Mike, what are you trying to say?"

"No, Mum, green *hair*!" said Mike. "That teacher at school isn't Mr. Prendergast. He looks like him but he's someone else entirely. Someone with yellow eyes, and – "

"And green hair," said his mother slowly. Suddenly, she started giggling. "What an imagination you have, Mike! Wait till your father hears this – what a laugh!"

"But, Mum, I'm serious," insisted Mike desperately. "Someone strange has taken the place of the real Mr. Prendergast. It's some kind of plot, I tell you!"

"And I'm telling you that I saw Mr. Prendergast outside the school at lunchtime today, when I was doing some shopping. I can assure you that he has blue eyes and grey hair, because he stopped to say hello."

"That's just it," cried Mike. "I'm the only one who can

see it. None of the others in my class noticed, any more than you did!"

"Well, there you are then," said his mother comfortably. For her, the argument was settled.

It was no good; Mike knew his parents would never believe him unless they saw for themselves. "You think I'm making it up, don't you?" he said miserably.

"I'll tell you what *I* think, young man. I think you're watching too much T.V. these days. Now, for heaven's sake, get on with your tea and let's forget about Mr. Prendergast. Perhaps," she added kindly, "you saw him in a peculiar light."

Mike wasn't convinced. The incident in the shed had been too frightening. That night he found it hard to sleep because he kept thinking of the weird teacher. Suppose he was imagining things? Perhaps his mother was right and the dull light in the shed had played tricks on his eyes. In that case, why had Mr. Prendergast seemed so uneasy? At last Mike dropped into a restless sleep, full of dreams through which green-haired, yellow-eyed strangers wandered as if they were lost in a foreign land, and paused occasionally to turn to him and whisper, "Why are you staring at me, boy? Who am I?"

The next day Mr. Prendergast took them for English. He didn't usually, but Miss Brown was off with 'flu. They had been reading some of Edward Lear's verse, and Mr. Prendergast asked them each to describe an imaginary land.

Mike was ready when his turn came. Screwing up his courage, he got to his feet.

"In my imaginary land, the country is very bare and rocky, and the people look very much like us."

The class listened, and Mr. Prendergast nodded encouragingly, rooting in his desk for a pen.

"Very much like us," Mike continued, "except – they all have yellow eyes and green hair."

There was a tremendous crash as Mr. Prendergast's desk slammed shut. White-faced, the teacher stared at Mike. A tense silence fell, and Jill Jones giggled nervously.

"What did you say?" Mr. Prendergast tried to remain calm, but his voice was trembling.

"I said, yellow eyes and green – "

"That will do. Very good, Mike. Next!"

Jimmy, glancing in some surprise from Mike to the

teacher, stood up and began his description. Mike sat down. He found that he, too, was shaking, but more than anything he felt triumphant. Mr. Prendergast's reaction had proved he was right. Something strange *was* happening – but Mike still had to find out exactly what. The worrying thing was that now he had come out into the open, Mr. Prendergast would be on his guard. Somehow Mike had to find out more about him while appearing not to suspect anything at all. From now on, he had to act innocent. That would be difficult, he realised. Mr. Prendergast was looking at him uneasily, with a weird expression in his wide yellow eyes.

After the lesson the teacher stopped to talk to him.

"That was a curious idea of yours, lad, about the people with – with green hair," he said. "What made you think of that?"

"Perhaps I dreamed it, sir," Mike answered, as truthfully as he could.

"Oh, indeed? That's very interesting," said Mr. Prendergast. His eyes narrowed. "Of course, there could be no such people . . . could there?"

"Well, you never know, sir. They have even stranger things on television."

"Ah… television," the teacher repeated. "Do you watch a lot of T.V.? Care for a bar of chocolate, by the way?"

"No thank you, sir," Mike replied, edging away. "It's playtime now," he hinted.

"So it is. Run along then," said Mr. Prendergast, and Mike gladly obeyed. He no longer trusted Mr. Prendergast, however friendly the teacher might appear to be.

Over the weekend, Mike made a plan. He decided to see what the man who called himself Mr. Prendergast did in the evenings. It would be easy enough to slip away to the teacher's house after supper for an hour or two and find out whether he spent his time marking books and reading, as he used to before – before what? What had caused the change? Mike pondered the teasing, nagging question. To give him the benefit of the doubt, Mr. Prendergast might, of course, be ill. Maybe he'd had yellow jaundice or something, which could explain his eyes; but not, surely, his hair? Perhaps he'd banged his head and lost his memory. If so, why did he remember some things, and seem unsure about others?

What if he were a Russian spy, planted in Britain to steal

secrets? That might be possible, but what secrets would a teacher in a small school steal that would be worth anything to an enemy? No, none of that made any sense. It's something else, thought Mike, something sinister, something I'll have to discover on my own.

The following evening found him crouched behind the privet hedge outside Mr. Prendergast's house. From where he was stationed, Mike could see quite clearly across the lawn and into the lounge. Fortunately the curtains were not drawn, though dusk was gathering.

A T.V. set was flickering away unheeded in a corner, and Mr. Prendergast was marking pages, and he worked his way through the pile of exercise books with what seemed to Mike to be unnatural speed. When he had finished, he yawned, stretched, and turned his attention to the television. Mike shifted uncomfortably in his cramped position, and changed his mind about being a James Bond type of spy when he grew up. Just as he was beginning to feel that he was wasting his time, Mr. Prendergast glanced at his watch, stood up and reached for his coat.

This is it, thought Mike, and a tingle of excitement ran down his spine. He made sure that he and his bike were tucked out of sight, and waited for the teacher to come out of the house.

Mr. Prendergast looked round furtively, turned up his collar and began to walk quickly across the fields without once glancing back. He's making for the woods! Mike thought, his heart racing. As quietly as he could he got up and began to follow Mr. Prendergast, wheeling his bike soundlessly along the grassy paths.

When they reached Bluebell Wood, named for its carpet of blue flowers in the spring, Mike propped his bicycle against a tree and followed Mr. Prendergast, flitting stealthily in and out of the trees and keeping well behind him. He had no fear of getting lost; he knew every path of Bluebell Wood.

Mr. Prendergast was making for the centre where the trees were thickest. Mike could hear the crackle of his feet on the autumn leaves, and he could just make out the dim striding shape of the man before him. He stopped in a little clearing, and Mike dodged behind a tree to watch.

Out of his pocket Mr. Prendergast took a thin metal object, which he held above his head. A steady whine, like the sound of bees, filled the air. Then suddenly there was a rumble, and the ground underfoot began to tremble. Mike clutched the tree, wide-eyed, as the noise grew louder and the earth heaved and split in the centre of the clearing; a great, shining white dome rose into view. The whine stopped. A triangular-shaped door in the dome slid back, and into the clearing stepped the strangest-looking man Mike had ever seen.

He was very tall, and dressed in a pale gold suit. His hair shone silvery-green in the moonlight. *A spaceman*, thought Mike. These people are from another world!

The two began to talk in low voices, and he inched forward to listen.

"All goes well with the Project, Toren," said the man in the golden suit. "How are things progressing with you?"

"I believe the Earth-boy suspects," said the man Mike knew as Mr. Prendergast.

"Then he must not be allowed to tell of his suspicions. Remember, nothing and nobody must interfere with Project 9! This boy – "

Just then Mike, moving forward, trod on a dry branch and fell. The noise was like the crack of doom in the quiet clearing. Mike glimpsed the angry face of Mr. Prendergast as he whirled round, and then he was off, running like a deer through the dark wood. At the edge of the trees he found his bicycle. He flung himself on to the saddle and rode home as fast as he could.

Project 9! People from another planet! Perhaps they were planning a war, an invasion, the destruction of the world! Mike went to bed feeling desperate. There was no-one to tell, for he was sure that no-one would ever believe him. Even if the clearing in Bluebell Wood were dug up, the spaceship, or base, or whatever the white dome-shaped thing was, probably wouldn't be found. The Project 9 people's technology was obviously too advanced for them to be caught like that. To confront 'Mr. Prendergast' would be a waste of time also; everyone else saw a respectable, well-established, grey-haired teacher instead of the humanoid alien Mike could see.

By the next morning, however, he had made a plan. Who would listen to him but the newspapers? He decided to write to the *Daily Argus*, which specialised in sensational stories and headlines. They might think he was crazy – but on the other hand maybe, just maybe, they would send a reporter to check. Reporters were famous for tracking down mysteries and making 'scoops' out of them, and if the paper managed to reveal this story he was sure it would make a scoop-and-a-half, and sell a lot of newspapers into the bargain!

He bought a *Daily Argus* on the way to school the next morning, and sidled off to the school library with some notepaper, instead of going to his lessons. *"Dear Editor,"* he began . . .

By ten o'clock he had finished the account of his strange experiences. He folded up the letter and slotted it into its envelope. He was licking the flap when a black shadow fell across the table. Mike knew who it was at once; and sure enough he looked up into the weird face of Mr. Prendergast.

"You should be in class, Michael," Mr. Prendergast murmured, but he wasn't really concerned with Mike's absence. He was staring at the envelope, his eyes glowing with a frightening golden gleam. He seemed to be *reading* the letter inside, which was impossible, unless he had X-ray eyes! This dreadful idea was confirmed when the teacher reached for the envelope. "May I have that?" He snatched for it, but Mike was quicker.

Clutching his letter tightly he made a dash for the door. There was a pillarbox over the road from the school, and once outside he flew across the playground as if he were racing in a marathon, with Mr. Prendergast close on his heels. A sixty-year-old man running as fast as a boy! And almost catching up with him! As he rounded a corner he felt a bony hand grabbing his shoulder, and then –

"Oops! Sorry, sir!" Mike gasped as he collided with the tall figure of the headmaster.

Mr. Jenkins frowned. "What's the hurry, Michael?"

"Just going to post a letter, sir," Mike gasped, holding up his envelope for proof.

"Well, there's no need to rush. The post isn't collected for half an hour yet. Be careful crossing the road. Ah, Mr. Prendergast, just the chap. I wanted a word with you."

While the Head talked to the helpless Mr. Prendergast, Mike hurried to the post box. Glancing back he could see his teacher watching him, his large eyes glaring in a golden blaze of fury.

For the next few days Mike was on pins, waiting for

some reaction to his letter. He avoided the alien as much as possible in the meantime.

The following Friday a parcel arrived from the *Daily Argus*. Mike ripped it open in great excitement to read the letter inside.

"Dear Michael," he read. "We are very pleased to tell you that you have won third prize in our Great Under-Fifteens' Science Fiction Story Competition . . ."

Mike crumpled the letter while his parents exclaimed over his prize, which was a camera. He hadn't even known that the newspaper was running a competition.

He felt quite defeated as he took his place in class that morning. Mr. Prendergast strolled in and glanced at him with what Mike thought was a triumphant sneer. He clenched his fists in anger.

Somehow, he was sure, the teacher knew about the newspaper's having mistaken his urgent letter for an entry in their competition. He could do nothing, and meanwhile the alien creature was sauntering among them, plotting heaven knew what with his awful friends, and nobody would take warning because they would never in a million years believe Mike's story! Mr. Prendergast was quite safe.

"Any questions about yesterday's science lesson, Form II?" asked the teacher casually.

Scowling, Mike got to his feet. "Yes, sir. What is Project 9?"

Just for a second the teacher, caught off-guard, went pale. Then he laughed.

"Project 9? Whatever are you talking about, Michael? Have you been watching too much television again?"

The class giggled. Mike sat down in a silent rage. If only he had some proof, some evidence . . . evidence! The camera! That was it – if he could photograph the space-ship and the spaceman in the woods with Mr. Prendergast, they'd have to believe him then! His father could show the photograph to the police and the newspapers and they would *have* to start an investigation! Mike was trembling with excitement inside, but for the rest of the day he tried to look downcast and beaten. Once or twice he saw Mr Prendergast looking at him with a satisfied smile. We'll see who has the last laugh, thought Mike grimly.

He couldn't wait to get home, though he knew that he had a dangerous evening's work in front of him. After he had taken the picture he would have to get out of Bluebell

91

Woods as quickly and quietly as possible, for the flash bulb on the camera would warn the aliens of his presence. When they'd had tea that evening his father showed him how to set the camera so that it would take snaps in the dusk, and Mike rode off to Mr. Prendergast's house to wait until he came out.

Eventually, looking for all the world like a pleasant elderly gentleman out for his evening stroll, Mr. Prendergast appeared. Keeping well out of sight, Mike tracked him to the clearing in the wood. He crouched behind a bush and quickly adjusted his camera as Mr. Prendergast held out the buzzing metal instrument he carried and, with a tremor that shook the ground, the great white dome began slowly to rise from the bowels of the earth.

The triangular door slid back, and out stepped the man in the golden suit. Mr. Prendergast moved towards him, Mike raised the camera and pressed the button –

"Stay where you are."

The voice was quiet, but full of authority. Mike turned, and there in front of him stood another alien, yellow-eyed and green-haired like the rest, dressed in a space-suit of silvery-blue material. "Come," he said, and pointed towards the dome.

Mike's first thought was to run, but the alien grasped his arm with fingers of steel, and he saw that it was useless to resist. Still clutching his camera, he was led across the clearing.

The first thing Mr. Prendergast did was to seize the camera and expose Mike's film. He turned towards the boy, his brows gathered in a ferocious scowl.

"So, you followed me! You must forget about Project 9, or it will be the worse for you!"

"No, Toren," said the golden-suited man. "It is impossible to scare him off – this boy will never give up. I fear we will have to take him with us, and show him what we are about."

"Explain Project 9?" gasped Mr. Prendergast – Toren, as they called him. "Is that wise, Skura?"

"We have no choice," replied the man named Skura gravely. "Take him to the Dome."

Mike began to struggle and yell as their strong hands fastened on him, but then he felt a tiny pinprick in his arm and everything went black.

When he came to, the world looked different. Drowsily

Mike blinked at a cloudless blue sky from a comfortable, feathery bed. It took some minutes to wake fully, and during that time he became aware of being in a glass room, looking out at a fresh new world. Trees and plants, the like of which he had never seen before, grew luxuriously outside. Birds twittered in the distance and people with pale green hair and golden eyes, dressed in different-coloured suits of silvery material, strolled along sandy paths. They smiled and waved when they saw him. A leopard-like animal with a lion's head ambled up to the clear wall and regarded him curiously. Mike shrank back, but it only yawned and trotted off among the passers-by, who seemed quite unafraid.

Then the door opened and Skura walked in, closely followed by – *two* Mr. Prendergasts! One was his old teacher, and the other . . . had green hair.

"Don't be scared, Michael. Everything's all right," said Skura.

"Hello, Mike, it's good to see you again." The real Mr. Prendergast grinned and clapped him on the shoulder. Mike couldn't speak for astonishment; he felt as though he were dreaming. "Now, don't worry about a thing. Watch Toren!"

The false Mr. Prendergast raised his hands to his neck and slowly began to peel off the face mask which had made him look exactly like the man he had been impersonating. He stood revealed as a very young man with a friendly face.

"But why – how . . . ?" stammered Mike.

"We'll tell you why and how, all in good time," chuckled Mr. Prendergast. "First of all, how about a little refreshment?"

He pointed to a tray on which there were cakes and fizzy drinks. Mike tasted them, cautiously at first, and found them sweet and delicious. Feeling much better, he asked, "Where are we?"

"This is the Planet Xenis," said Skura, "and you will be wondering what we Xenites are doing on Planet Earth. I will tell you. The fact is that Xenis is far older than your world. There has been life on Earth for only a few million years, as Time goes, whereas we have been in existence for much longer. Our race has therefore progressed further than yours."

"Everyone certainly looks very happy," said Mike doubtfully, gazing at the contented people strolling by.

"We are," said Skura. "We have everything we want, and so we decided, aeons ago, that we would find developing worlds and help them with their technology so that they, too, might be happy."

"They are a very gentle people," explained Mr. Prendergast. "It troubles them to see the misery in younger worlds like ours."

"Then why didn't you simply land on Earth and explain that you wanted to help?" demanded Mike. "Instead of – "

"Instead of sending me to impersonate Mr. Prendergast," Toren finished. "Think, Michael. Can't you imagine the panic we would have caused? Aliens from another planet arriving out of the blue – your people would have been frightened out of their wits. I'm afraid I gave *you* some awful scares, by the way, and I'm very sorry for that. But we had to safeguard Project 9. Yours, by the way, is the ninth planet we have chosen to help – hence the name."

"I see," said Mike. "It was a good thing nobody believed me when I tried to tell them you weren't Mr. Prendergast! And of course," he added, turning to his teacher, "you knew all about this?"

"Yes," said Mr. Prendergast. "Like you, I had an awful shock when I first saw Toren, with his golden eyes and green hair. Then he explained what the Xenites were planning to do, and of course I agreed to aid them by swapping places."

"So we brought Mr. Prendergast here during the school holidays to examine the way he, as a typical Earthman, thinks," Skura resumed. "We have to find that out, you see, so that we will know how to suggest new ideas to your race. What we did was to record his memory and personality in our computers, and then feed them into Toren's brain. We made him a face-mask, landed him on Earth, and – hey presto! Another Mr. Prendergast! It worked quite well, though Toren did slip up once or twice, as you cleverly noticed."

"Meanwhile," Toren continued, "Skura and his team burrowed our Base – the white dome you saw – into the ground to do experiments with your soil and plants. Already," he added proudly, "we have developed a way of trebling your food production. Also, we have been examining your rather primitive monetary systems, and we think that we can make things better all round, eventually."

"So there won't be any more disasters?" said Michael.

"Not if we're successful," smiled Skura. "We will find a way of putting our solutions to your problems into the brains of your rulers and scientists, so that in the future there won't be any more wars or famines or . . . any of that." The Xenite shuddered as he mentioned these tragedies.

"That's wonderful," said Mike. "How long will it take?"

"We aren't sure yet," replied Skura. "We should finish examining Mr. Prendergast in a couple of weeks and then we'll send him back to Earth. From then on we can begin Stage Two, which means we start our improvements."

"I shall be sorry to leave," murmured Mr. Prendergast. "It's marvellous here."

"Thank you," said Skura. "You will be welcome here any time you choose to come. And now we must all get back to Earth, otherwise you will be missed, Michael, and so will 'Mr. Prendergast'."

"Gosh! How long have I been here?" asked Mike.

"Six hours of our time, and half an hour of yours, at a rough calculation," answered Skura. "I'm afraid we'll have to put you to sleep again for the journey back, Michael. If you aren't used to time travel, it can be pretty exhausting."

Mr. Prendergast shook hands with Mike.

"Goodbye, sir," said Mike. "I'll see you in a couple of weeks."

"Take care, sonny," said Mr. Prendergast. "You've been very brave. I'm proud of you."

On the way to Skura's spaceship Mike said, "There's just one more question I'd like to ask. Why is it that I could see the real Toren, and nobody else could?"

"We don't know," confessed Skura. "There are still a lot of things about Earth people that we don't know. Let's just say . . . that you can see clearer than most people."

Inside the great silver spaceship Mike was put into a deep sleep. When he woke up he was standing outside his house, and Toren, again looking like Mr. Prendergast, was with him.

"See you at school tomorrow, Michael," he said with a wink. "Don't be late!"

"I won't," Mike promised. "Goodnight, Tor – Mr. Prendergast!"

He let himself into his house, suddenly feeling very tired.

"We were just getting worried about you, Mike," said

his father. "You were out late tonight. Where have you been?"

"Well," said Mike, "I was taken to the Planet Xenis in a spaceship to help with Project 9, and – "

"Oh, honestly, Mike! What an imagination you've got!" laughed his mother.

"And what's Project 9?" joked his father.

Mike grinned. "You wouldn't believe me if I told you," he said.

A CROCODILE EGG

by JOHN HALKIN

Almost everyone living in the Main Dome on Planet Rit-10 has pieces of crocodile egg somewhere around their living quarters so I'd no real reason to feel uneasy when Chuck brought a whole one back to camp that evening. Yet an odd sort of shiver went through me the moment he took it out of his bag and placed it on the rickety camp table.

"What d'you think of it?" Dad asked after a few seconds' awkward silence. "Owen?"

"It's . . . great," I answered, trying to hide my lack of enthusiasm. The trouble was I liked Chuck, we all did, and didn't want to disappoint him. "Yeah, it's really great, isn't it, Teg?"

"A bit ordinary, though," my brother said. "Couldn't you find a nicer one? Or were they sold out?"

Dad flushed angrily. "Chuck risked his life getting that egg."

"Oh, the boys are right!" Chuck declared as he struggled to pull off his respirator; as usual, the straps had become entangled in his wild red hair. "Ouch! I'll be bald before I'm much older! Just look at that – five hairs I've lost this time!"

Teg grinned at him. "Try having a haircut," he suggested cheekily.

Chuck laughed. "Anyway, about this egg. It doesn't look much, I know, but it's different from any other croc egg you've ever seen. Can you guess why?"

It was speckled – but then they often are – and its colours

96

were nothing to signal Earth about, just a dull brown-and-white, with blackish spots. At home we had a flower bowl made of emerald and cream shell segments which glowed when the lights were low, and one of our neighbours had a collection of brilliant red and blue shells. Yet, as I stared at this one, I had that strange feeling again and knew there must be something very unusual about it.

Teg, in one of his teasing moods, was walking around the egg, looking at it from every side. "Has it got legs? I think it must have legs tucked away underneath. That's what it is, Chuck – the original walking egg. Easy!"

"Oh, don't be so stupid, Teg!" I snapped at him impatiently. There were times my younger brother really got on my nerves and it was a mystery to me why Chuck ever put up with him. "Don't you *see*?"

"See what?"

"It's alive!" As I spoke I could almost visualise a fully-formed baby croc moving around inside, getting bigger every second, waiting for the right moment to break out. "That's it, isn't it?" I appealed to Chuck.

He nodded.

"But won't it die?"

"Hard to say, it's early days yet. That egg was only laid three hours ago. I disturbed the mother – not that I wanted to, it's not the sort of risk I like taking – and had to use my laser to save my own life. Probably only stunned her, though."

"I'm glad you didn't kill her."

"It's kill or be killed in that sort of situation more often than not. As for the egg, I think the best thing is to put it into deep freeze till we get back to the Dome." He turned to Dad who was beginning to unpack the things for our evening meal. "What do you think?"

"No-one's yet hatched out a croc in our atmosphere," Dad said, "and the chances are it'd choke to death even if you did succeed. The nitrogen content of the air down in the swamps is even higher than up here, and as that's the crocs' natural habitat, they're probably dependent on it."

"Oh, I hope he lives, then I can keep him as a pet!" Teg cried out, looking at the egg more closely. He leaned his elbows on the camp table and cupped his chin in his hands. "I'll be the only person in the Dome with a pet crocodile. Oh, I do hope he lives, Dad, 'cos he *is* mine, isn't he? I mean, I was the one who asked Chuck to get a croc egg, so that makes him mine, doesn't it?"

Dad ran his fingers through Teg's hair. "We'll see about that," he laughed. "But don't you think Mum'd better be consulted? Let's have something to eat before it's time to make video contact with her. She'll want to know what you've been doing all day *and* how you like camping outside the Dome."

Though I said nothing at the time it worried me that I seemed to be the only one who felt at all uneasy about the egg. Not that I expected Dad to notice anything; he was a surveyor and had no use for anything which couldn't be measured and described in strict scientific terms. Chuck, his assistant, was the same. And that's understandable enough if you live on a hostile planet whose air is so deadly to human beings that they've had to construct a giant transparent dome over the whole settlement and fill it with an artificially-controlled atmosphere. Under those circumstances what you need is common-sense and practical solutions, not mysteries.

And the egg was a mystery.

In fact, to me at that moment everything outside the Dome was a mystery and I was surprised Teg didn't feel the same. We'd grown up hearing only the steady hum of the air-conditioners and here we were, outside for the first time, and he chattered away as though none of it made any impression on him whatsoever. He was only eight, of course, though that's no excuse. To me, "outside" was like a thousand voices whispering their secrets, with the call of unseen animals, birds, insects, and the rustle of wind through the leaves.

And now the egg. Though I knew Chuck had put it safely away in one of the deep freeze specimen containers, I could still sense something emanating from it, almost as if it were transmitting a signal which my mind couldn't decode, however hard I tried.

As I lay in my sleeping bag in the pressurized atmos-controlled tent I suddenly thought I heard a sound closer than all the rest and I propped myself up on my elbow to look around. Chuck and Dad were absorbed in their work at the far end. Teg was asleep.

Yes, there it was again! A noise, coming from several sides.

"Dad," I said urgently.

"What's the matter, Owen? Can't you sleep? Try to sleep, there's a good boy." He went back to his calculations.

"But, Dad, listen . . . outside . . ."

"Oh, that's only the wind in the . . ." He broke off as we heard it again, much louder this time. "Sounds like something's moving around the site," he said to Chuck. "We'd best have the lights on and investigate."

Chuck touched a switch on the N-generator and the walls of the tent suddenly glowed white as the ring of external lights came on. I'd helped him to fix them up earlier in the day and he'd explained how these high-intensity lamps were our main defence against marauding animals. "Effective, too," he'd told me. "Scares 'em off. Fear's always the best weapon, lad. Remember that." But I couldn't help wondering what'd happen if they weren't frightened by the light. What could four of us – two men, two boys – do against a really determined herd of . . . I shuddered when I thought of some of the beasts roaming around outside.

Dad pulled his respirator on and picked up his laser gun. "Stay in the tent, Owen. There's nothing to worry about." He waited till Chuck was ready and they went out together.

I sat on my sleeping bag, straining my ears to try and understand what was going on, but apart from the screech of a bird in the distance I heard nothing. Teg was still asleep, oblivious of everything.

At last I could stand the silence no longer. I went across to the box where the respirators were kept. Chuck had already changed the filters, and I put mine on. There was no point in staying inside, I decided.

I slipped out through the double flaps of the atmos-lock and found myself blinking furiously to accustom my eyes to the brightness of the lamps. The trees looked oddly white against the black sky and down the hill a spread of pale mist merged with the darkness.

"Thought I told you to stay in the tent," said Dad, his voice muffled by the respirator. "Keep back in the shadows."

"I wanted to know what was happening."

"Nothing's happening. If there was an animal here it scarpered when the lights came on."

"There was more than one," I insisted. "I heard them, Dad. They were all round the tent."

"Maybe. Maybe not. More likely your imagination. Take
99

after your mother, you do, Owen. Head full of dreams. Come on, let's go back in." He called out to Chuck. "Have a scout round, will you? We're going inside. But leave the lights on, I think. No point in taking risks."

When I was back in my sleeping bag he came and sat down beside me. "You know, Owen, the biggest danger on an expedition is getting at cross-purposes with your mates. I told you to stay in the tent, didn't I?"

"Yes, Dad, but . . ."

"Now, listen, Owen, you've got to obey orders. Let's say Chuck or I had seen a movement out there in the shadows near the tent, just out of the corner of the eye, without really knowing what it was. Doesn't take a split second to swing round and shoot, and there are times you must do it to stay alive. But that movement could've been you .D'you understand what I'm saying?"

I said I did.

"It's happened before. A friend of mine was shot by a member of his own expedition, accidentally. Lost an arm, and lucky to get off so lightly." Dad stood up. "So now you know. Don't let it happen again, eh?"

"Dad, about that egg . . ." I tried, but he stopped me.

"You go to sleep now," he said firmly. "Nothing'll happen to the egg while it's in deep freeze."

"No, that's not what I mean. I wanted to tell you before, but . . ."

"Sleep!" he ordered, leaving me no alternative.

I turned over in my sleeping bag and closed my eyes.

The next morning I knew I'd been right about the animals having been all around the tent. The scratches in the soil were clearly visible, plants were flattened and several young trees had been broken. I glanced at Dad but he seemed determined not to mention the incident.

"We'll go down to that river you can see just beyond those rocks," he decided, pointing the place out. "It'll be nice for the boys to play there for a couple of hours while we get on with our work. Ready, Chuck?"

Teg was already racing ahead and I ran after him, shouting that he mustn't get too far away from the rest of us. After last night's experience the world outside the Dome no longer seemed quite so attractive. But at least – the thought made me stop abruptly with shock – at least the egg was quiet. I hadn't felt it at all that morning, that menacing

100

sensation which'd been with me ever since Chuck'd first brought it into the tent. It was completely gone!

"Whoops!" I shouted with relief as the realisation struck me. "Look out, Teg! Bet you I'll get to the river first!"

"Bet you won't!"

We dashed down the slope. He was well in front of me but at last I managed to overtake him. I reached the river bank first, though only by a couple of metres. Then I threw myself down on the grass to get my breath back while Teg wandered off on his own. Looking back up the hill I could see Dad and Chuck coming down more carefully with the electronic theodolite and other instruments.

"Owen!" The sheer panic in Teg's voice hit me in the stomach like a clenched fist. "Owen, quick! Oh, do something!"

I turned to see him backing away from the river, terrified, as a giant yellow crocodile crawled through the reeds towards him.

"Run!" I yelled desperately. "Teg, run up the hill. You can get away from it. You *can*, Teg! Run!"

But he moved too slowly, as though hypnotised by those gleaming rows of teeth, until he collided with a massive tree-trunk and stopped. Then I saw two other crocodiles had emerged from the water, one on either side of him and I began to understand what was happening. Teg was being deliberately ambushed!

Laser shots from Dad and Chuck burned into the surrounding trees as they tried to scare the crocodiles away. But the biggest, his ugly eyes bulging crimson in his mottled yellow head, lifted his snout and bellowed in triumph before seizing Teg in his powerful jaws and turning swiftly towards the river again.

I *had* to do something, I just couldn't stand there watching, so I conceived the crazy idea of trying to snatch Teg back from those awful shining teeth; but as I bounded forward I was gripped by one of the others, lifted high into the air and shaken backwards and forwards, backwards and forwards till I stopped struggling.

I heard more shots from Dad and Chuck but they gradually receded as the crocodiles carried us downstream in the direction of the swamp.

From time to time I caught glimpses of Teg as he lay white and still in the giant crocodile's jaws. "Teg!" I tried to shout across to him. "Teg, do something! Kick!" But either he was unconscious or my voice was too weak to be heard. My own captor's teeth bit into me just beneath the ribs, making it difficult to breathe.

But why were we still alive? From all I'd heard of crocodiles, they usually ate first and asked questions afterwards. Yet they seemed more intent on taking us prisoner. No-one'd ever suggested there were intelligent life forms on Rit-10, least of all crocodiles.

Then, as we neared the swamp, an overhanging branch accidentally caught in the straps of Teg's respirator and tugged it off. "He'll die!" I screamed though I knew it was useless, nobody could help. "Oh, he'll die without his respirator. Do something!"

The crocodiles stopped and one of them reached up to pluck the respirator down from the branch with his teeth. I don't know if you've ever been terrified and astonished simultaneously but this is just what I felt when I saw what they were doing. *These reptiles were trying to pull the respirator over Teg's head!*

They were too clumsy and it slipped off again.

"You do it!" I was ordered. The words formed themselves in my brain without having been spoken. *"He must not die. We need him."*

Before I was able to grasp what was happening I'd been dropped roughly on the ground.

Teg was fighting for breath, painfully, gulping in great mouthfuls of the poisonous air; his face was already swollen and unnatural. I managed to get the respirator over his head and held him steady as I pulled the straps into place. At last he began to breathe more quietly and even opened his eyes for a moment and spoke to me – just my name, nothing else – but he fainted again when he saw the crocodiles around us.

"Come!"

They're communicating with us, I tried to tell myself; I don't believe this; it's just not happening; it's a dream, a bad dream . . .

But they picked us both up once more and carried us deep into the swamp to a small island where they almost threw us down, wet and exhausted. I struggled to sit up but Teg just lay there, moaning. The giant crocodile waddled around us, flicking his tail dangerously. Then he stopped in front of Teg and pushed at the respirator with his snout.

"This helps him to live?"

Once again the question seemed to arise in my mind without any sound being made. I'd read about human experiments in telepathy and how most of them had failed, but if these reptiles could use it to convey coherent messages . . . I tried to 'think' an answer without actually saying the words but the only result was that the question repeated itself impatiently.

"This helps him to live?"

"Yes, it's an air filter," I said aloud. I don't think the crocodile listened to my voice but I'd the impression that the act of speaking somehow strengthened the mental signal I was transmitting. "Its effect lasts for about twelve hours, then it has to be changed."

I knew my answer had got through to him for the next sensation was like having a big question mark in my skull. I'd given the right answer all right, but he hadn't understood a word of it. I tried to explain. "Until nightfall . . ."

A drifting mist covered the swamp, blurring the outlines of the trees which stood high above the water on tall, leg-like roots. Among them I spotted eyes observing us and gradually became aware that hundreds of crocodiles surrounded the island, waiting, watching, and occasionally opening their great jaws to reveal luminescent white teeth.

Yet now we could speak to each other, however simply, I was no longer quite so afraid.

"What d'you want?"

As soon as I'd spoken I knew the answer myself. "The egg?"

Suddenly the water around us became alive as the crocodiles swung their tails excitedly and snapped their jaws. Only the giant who'd carried Teg remained calm, looking almost lazily at me. No words formed themselves in my head this time but I sensed well enough what thought he was transmitting. We were entirely in his power and he'd not hesitate to kill both of us if any harm came to the egg.

But it took a long time for me to understand exactly what they wanted. Only the simplest ideas seemed to get through. At first I imagined stupidly that no Rit-10 reptile could possibly be as intelligent as a human being from Earth. But slowly I began to realise the truth: it wasn't lack of intelligence causing the problems but the fact that our thought patterns were so different, we had to go over every point again and again to make sure we really knew what was meant.

To express it in our own Earth way, Teg was to be held hostage until the living egg was returned. I was made to understand there was something very special about the person to be born out of that egg, though they couldn't explain that. Whenever I mentioned words such as 'prince', 'king', or 'leader', they rejected them and we had to start all over again.

I told them repeatedly I was willing to stay as hostage in Teg's place, but they wouldn't accept me as being of equal value. Apparently – this was how I interpreted what they were trying to say – they could look into Teg's mind and spot something there which none of us had yet recognised, though I don't know what it was. Me they regarded as a messenger.

The giant crocodile must have sensed I felt hurt, and transmitted a puzzled question mark, as if he couldn't understand feelings of jealousy and rivalry.

"I'm the one who can communicate with you!" I pleaded with them. "Among human beings that's . . . well, it's unheard-of! No-one's managed telepathy before."

But the only response I got to that argument was bewilderment that I didn't understand my task – to go back to the tent, fetch the egg, and take it to the river bank. Why should I object once my role had been made clear?

So I agreed. I'd no alternative. As my captor's jaws closed around my middle again I was uncomfortably aware he'd only to tighten them a shade more and I'd end up broken in half. He slipped into the water and the nightmare journey back again. Teg stayed on the island, still hardly conscious.

I spotted Chuck first searching the river bank, maybe hoping to discover some evidence of what had happened to us. I've never in my life been so glad to see any sight so much as his mop of red hair and his friendly face breaking out into smiles.

"You're alive!" he cried out with genuine joy. "Owen, you're alive after all!" From the sound of his voice I knew he was finding it difficult to believe his own eyes. "And you're all right?"

"Yes, and so is Teg!" I told him eagerly. "We've only got to do what the crocodiles want and they'll bring him back to us."

Chuck looked at me questioningly, then put his arm round my shoulder. "I think we'd better get you back to camp. Get you out of those wet clothes and give you a sedative. Your Dad's up there now trying to break the news to your mother on the video. Oh, I'm so glad to see you, lad!"

It was then I began to feel how hopeless it all was. One look at Chuck's face and I knew he wouldn't believe me. "Communicate with crocodiles? He must be overwrought . . .!" And Dad's reaction would be the same, I was certain. They'd send for a helicopter, have me transferred back to the Dome, put in hospital . . . In the meantime Teg would die.

"We must take the egg down to the river," I attempted to explain for the fourth time.

"Yes, all right, Owen, you can tell us afterwards. Why don't you run on ahead and surprise your Dad?"

But the moment I stepped into the tent I knew what I had to do.

"Mum! Dad!" I shouted tearing off my respirator and dashing forward till I was within range of the video lens. "I'm all right! I'm alive, and so is Teg!" And I began to pour out the whole story of everything that'd happened, confident that Mum would insist on the right thing.

Of course I don't think she believed me, but I didn't worry about that so long as they let me take the egg down to the river. Chuck gave me a hot drink and some food while they argued about it on the video.

"The boy's delirious," Dad was saying. "He's probably got a fever, and it's no wonder after what he's been through."

"But if there's just a chance of it being true?" Mum sounded almost hysterical. "I know it's a ridiculous story, but . . . If you don't let him take that egg down to the river, I'll never forgive you!"

"All right," he gave way. "There's no harm in it, I suppose; but there's no good in it, either."

"Do it *now*."

I think Dad began to have doubts when he saw the masses of crocodiles assembled on the river bank, waiting for us. He told me I mustn't go anywhere near them, but leave the egg on the higher ground where we'd stopped. I shook my head and, holding the egg carefully out in front of me, I walked towards them. "Here it is!" I called out. "I kept my promise! Here's the egg!"

Without needing to be told, I knew exactly where they

wanted me to put it. Then I turned and the crocodiles moved aside to let me pass. Teg was sitting among the reeds, shivering. "What happened?" he asked plaintively. "I don't know what happened."

The crocodiles slid away into the river, all of them, taking the egg with them, and I went back with Teg, Dad and Chuck to the camp. The video link was still open and Mum cried with joy when she saw us all coming in.

I never found out what the crocodiles saw in Teg's mind, nor what was so special about that particular egg; they obviously have their own values which are very different from ours. And what's even more puzzling, they've never again tried to communicate, though I've been to the swamp several times since. That 'telepathic gift' of mine turned out to be non-existent; all the mental power came from them.

So that's the way it's remained. We respect their privacy and they don't bother us. We live side by side on the same planet and politely ignore each other. After all, they were the original inhabitants of Rit-10 and if they don't make the first move, what can we do about it?

THE MONSTER IN THE WOOD

by ROSEMARY TIMPERLEY

The wood had darkened. Tom began to hurry. He'd spent this Sunday going for a long walk with his friends and now he was later coming home than he should be. That was why he was taking the short cut through the wood. He was allowed to do this in the daytime, but not at night.

"Why not?" he'd asked his mother.

"Because there's a monster in the wood which comes out at night," she'd replied, poker-faced. Tom was never sure when she was teasing and when serious.

"You're kidding," he'd said.

"Well, don't walk through the wood at night just to prove it," was her enigmatic response, "or you might never be seen again. The monster would chop you up into little pieces and eat you."

106

"What's this monster like?"

"That would be telling."

She was maddening! If it wasn't, "that would be telling," it was "we'll see"; two of the most infuriating sentences ever invented to thwart children.

Now he began to run through the dark trees, more out of anxiety not to be too late and get into a row than because he believed in the monster – at least, that was the case until the big bush moved.

The big laurel bush. He knew it by sight. He'd passed it often enough by day when it stood meekly at the side of the path. But now, as he approached it, it stepped out in front of him.

Without a second thought, he turned and ran back the way he'd come. Then a voice called after him: "Please don't run away from me. I shan't hurt you. I need help."

It was a cultured, rather teacherish voice, and unhappy. Tom stopped running and looked round.

The big bush was still there across the path, but now a face was looking out from among the leaves. It was rather an old face with two white beards side by side, apparently growing on two chins, and very anxious eyes, two in the usual place, and a third in the middle of the forehead.

"Please come back. I'm in terrible trouble," the face said.

Tom thought anyone who looked like that was indeed in trouble, so he walked slowly back.

"Are you by any chance the monster?" he enquired.

"Don't be so cruel!" The three eyes filled with tears, and a tear from the middle eye rolled straight down the nose and dropped off the tip.

"Sorry," Tom said quickly. "Who are you then?"

"My name is Professor Turbelerian, and that name is at the root of my distress. If I'd been called Bloggs, Briggs or Candlewax I'd never have come to this."

"Come to what?" asked Tom.

"Well, look at me, child. You've already called me a monster."

"You do have rather a lot of features on your face," Tom said delicately, "but they're quite nice features. The hair of your beards is silky and you have three beautiful brown eyes."

"I grew my own extras," said the Professor with sad pride, "and now I'm landed with them and daren't show my face anywhere."

"Everyone grows their own limbs and features," said Tom. "They just happen to one. You can't help it."

"That applies to the standard number, not to the extras. When you grow additional bits and pieces, you *can* help it. I found the secret chemistry of growing extra parts, you see, and used myself as a guinea-pig. The result is that I have to live here in hiding, dressed in this bush. At first I didn't dare move, but I've pulled up the roots so that at least I can shift around in my bush, like a snail with leaves instead of a shell."

"Good thing it's an evergreen," Tom said practically, "or the leaves would have dropped off by now. In time they'll drop off anyway, if you've uprooted the thing. It'll die round you."

"Then I shall have to find another. I'll denude the whole wood in time – unless someone helps me."

At this point Tom didn't see how he could help. He could hardly take a three-eyed face in a bush back home with him – his mother would have a fit. So, to take the creature's mind off asking for help, he asked: "What gave you the idea of growing extra features in the first place?"

"My own name, of course: Turbelerian. I've explained that. I'm a professor of biology, chemistry, bio-chemistry, anthropology and other magic. I know all about worms, especially the one I'm named after, the turbelerian flat-worm."

He wiped his three eyes, scratched one of his bearded chins, took a twig with a ladybird on it out of the other beard, and continued.

"The turbelerian flatworm can be cut into pieces and each piece grows again into a complete organism. What's your name?"

"Tom Blake."

"Well, if you were a turbelerian flatworm and I cut you into a dozen pieces, after a while there'd be twelve little Tom Blakes. These worms do it all by themselves and I determined to find out what makes them tick – not what they do – they make a snuffling noise, and you can only hear that if you put them in front of a microphone which enlarges the sound. I watched and listened and chopped and experimented, and at last I found and synthesised the ingredient in their make-up which allows them to grow selves, as it were."

"Bully for you," said Tom, to please the Professor.

"I'm not a bully at all," he said indignantly. "I asked some of my students if they'd allow themselves to be chopped up and have the turbelerian ingredient injected into them, but they refused. Far from bullying them into it, I accepted the rebuff and used myself. However, I didn't chop myself up, in case the experiment failed, but I did adapt the ingredient so that I could grow new features on myself. As you can see, I succeeded. I was so happy and excited! I'd lived like a recluse while working, but now I came out into the world again, to be hailed as a great discoverer. I expected a Nobel Prize at least."

"You should have had one too," said Tom warmly. "It must have taken a lot of guts to do what you did."

"How good to be appreciated at last!" The three eyes dropped three more tears, and another big drop fell off the tip of the nose. "No one else appreciated what I'd done. Some ran away from me in terror. Some threw stones. A fairground owner tried to catch me for a freak show. I was on the run for weeks till I came to hide here. A freak show – imagine – "

"Terrible," agreed Tom. "Anyway, you have a nice face. It's only – er – different. And that that third eye must be useful for looking with."

"I have a fourth one at the back of my head, for seeing behind me," admitted Professor Turbelerian. "It's useful when there's danger, but annoying when I cry. The water trickles down the back of my neck. And then, Tom, my face isn't my only misfortune. Would that it were! I could go around in a Guy Fawkes mask or something. There's the rest of me."

"More extra bits?" said Tom. "May I see?"

"You're sure there's nobody around?"

"Not a soul. Come on out. We can put the bush back over you if we hear anyone coming."

Leaves and branches parted and the Professor stepped out of the bush. At first he looked ordinary enough, but for his three-eyed, two-chinned face, because he was wrapped in a muddy old blanket such as any man sleeping rough might wear.

He said: "I didn't grow any extra legs, thank goodness, so I can still wear my trousers, but my new arms are a problem."

He took off the blanket, revealing a lean torso with three rather skinny arms on either side.

"The middle two are the originals," he explained, folding his middle arms, while the lower two hung down by his side and he held out the upper two, like wings.

It was an awe-inspiring sight. He really was a monster, yet not ugly or frightening.

"I know what you're like," said Tom. "Those old statues of Hindu gods with lots of extra arms. They have more than six, though, otherwise you could have gone to India and been worshipped instead of having stones thrown at you and being called a freak. Can you use them all, or are the extras just decoration?"

"Oh, I can use them all. They were very handy, in every sense of the word, when I was uprooting this bush. I did it three times as fast as if I'd had only two. It's a wonderful thing I've done, you know, if only people appreciated it, but they're all so limited."

"You'd be worth your weight in gold as a fruit-picker," said Tom. "Or how about being a typist? You could use three typewriters at once – or play three pianos at once – or be a six-armed bandit with a gun in each hand – bang-bang-bang-bang-bang-bang – "

"I cannot type, play the piano or shoot," said the Professor irritably. "I want genuine help from you, not idiotic suggestions."

"How can I help? I would like to."

"I need something to make me look normal again, so I can show my face to the world."

"Yes," said Tom. "We've got to dress you up so no one would guess that you're different. I must go home now or my mother will be fighting mad, but I'll give it a think and come back tomorrow."

"You're a good boy, Tom Blake," said the Professor. "I know you won't give me away or let me down."

Tom thought about the Professor's problem as he ran the rest of the way home. He thought about it while his mother was scolding him, so hardly heard a word she said, which was a good thing. He thought about it as he lay in bed later. He formed a plan.

He got to school early on Monday morning and sneaked along to the big hamper where they kept dressing-up things for school plays. He 'borrowed' a black cape, a black sombrero-type hat and a false white beard. There was a little first-aid box also in the hamper and he took some dressings, the sort that were put on gashed knees

110

"No one will know you've got more than two arms."

after playground falls. He bundled this lot into his locker and waited impatiently for the lunch hour. When it came, he grabbed the items from his locker and ran all the way to the wood. He found the big laurel bush sitting meekly by the path as if it had never moved in its life.

"Here I am," he said eagerly, and three brown eyes peered out in a welcoming way. "Hello, Professor Turbo Jet," he said. "I've brought your disguise so you can walk about among people again."

"You wonderful child! Come inside the bush and show me. I've broken away some of the inside branches so there's more room."

Tom entered the bush-hut and held out the items in the green gloaming. The Professor nodded and smiled.

"Now I'll fix you up. Keep still and leave it all to me," said Tom. He felt adult and responsible, as if the other were the child. Come to think of it, it was pretty childish to grow extra eyes, chin and arms and expect people to be pleased and give one a Nobel Prize. The Professor was a great big baby at heart.

Tom removed the blanket from the other's shoulders and wrapped the cape round him, hiding the six arms. He buttoned it down the front. "No one will know you've got more than two arms now as there are only two arm-slits to put your hands through, and as all the hands look the same, it won't matter which two you use," he said. "You can let your different pairs take it in turns. Full employment without overtime."

Then he fixed the false beard so it filled in the gap between the two bearded chins. "Now it just looks like one very wide white beard. You'll seem a bit fat-faced, I'm afraid, but then so do a lot of so-called normal people. Our headmaster's got a chin like a coal shovel."

He placed the hat on the Professor's head. "That's in case anyone notices the eye at the back. You can take it off when you're alone and want to see behind you. Or you could cut a very tiny hole in the back of your hat, if you liked."

Next he applied the medical dressing to the eye in the middle of the forehead. "The plaster is pinkish, so it hardly shows. People will only think you've got a cut or a wart or something. Lots of people go about with bits of plaster on them. Now, let's get out of this bush and I'll take a real look at you."

112

Obediently, Professor Turbelerian stepped into the open.
He looked a little eccentric, but no more than that. There
he stood, black-hatted, wide-faced, white-bearded, wearing
a rather dramatic cape, and with an inconspicuous bit of
plaster in the middle of his forehead.

"You look smashing," said Tom. "You'll get a few
glances, but only of interest and admiration."

"I feel half-blind with only two eyes to see with," said
the Professor.

"You can't have everything," said Tom. "You wanted
to look normal, and now you do – super-normal!"

"Really?"

"Honest! Let's walk along to the shops together, then
you can see yourself reflected in a shop window. You'll be
pleased. If we meet anyone I know, I'll say you're an actor
friend. Come on, Professor Turbo Jet."

"Why do you call me that?"

"It's nicer than your old name. The worm has turned
into a high flyer," said Tom, becoming poetic with elation.
He was really proud of his achievement.

They walked through the wood and out the other side.
When they reached the town, they turned along the nearest
shopping street. One or two people eyed the cloaked,
bearded figure walking with a schoolboy, but no one
showed any surprise, let alone horror.

"You see? It's worked!" whispered Tom, grabbing the
Professor's arm under the cape – and finding three. The
other gave him a friendly triple-nudge.

They paused before a shop window, and the Professor
surveyed his reflection.

"This get-up suits me," he said with wonder. "I look
quite distinguished."

He added, with a chuckle, "These extra arms are uncom-
monly useful. I can scratch myself in all sorts of places."

"Don't fidget with them too much," Tom warned him.
"As for the scratching, I expect you need a bath. I can just
picture you, with three flannels and three cakes of soap,
and the job done in a few seconds!"

"You are a good boy! One day I shall reward you for all
the help you've given me," said Professor Turberlerian,
growing emotional, and Tom said, "Please don't cry or
that plaster on your brow, and the back of your hat, will
get soggy."

The Professor controlled himself. He may be a monster of a kind but he's an old softie really, thought Tom.

"Where shall you live now you've left the bush?" Tom asked.

"At an hotel, at first anyway. I have money in my trouser pocket. Wait." He scrabbled and chinked under his cloak, then one of his right arms came through the slit, empty. He looked at it in a puzzled way. "It had two fifty pence pieces in it," he said.

"Maybe you used a different hand to get the money out," Tom whispered, very softly for fear passers-by heard.

"That's just what I have done." He withdrew the empty hand and another right hand came out, with the money.

"You *must* be careful about that sort of thing," Tom said, as he accepted the present. "Thanks ever so much. I must get back to school now. Best of luck!"

They shook hands (which hand, top, middle or lower? thought Tom), and he ran back to school, leaving the Professor still admiring his new image in the shop window.

It was years later that Tom, almost grown-up now and about to leave school, received a cheque for a thousand pounds. With it was a letter: *"Dear Tom, I told you I would reward you one day for the way you helped me when many boys would have been frightened or repelled. Now at last I can do it handsomely. Remember me? With pride, I sign myself, TURBO JET THE MAGICIAN."*

"Turbo Jet the Magician?" said his mother, when he showed her the cheque. "But when did you help *him*?"

"Ages ago. When I was a kid. He wasn't famous then."

"Well, he's famous now, Tom. He's a rich and successful entertainer – magic and conjuring. He wears a black cloak and a tall hat, and a black star in the middle of his forehead, as a gimmick. He travels the world, baffling people with his sleight-of-hand and ability to see what's going on behind him."

"He must have cut a hole in the back of his hat, as I suggested," said Tom.

"What *do* you mean?" asked his mother.

"That," said Tom, "would be telling."

FROM THE DEEPS

by WENDY EYTON

Helen breathed deeply the clear and salty air, the hungry cry of seagulls in her ears. The tide was far out and she could hardly see beyond the stretches of flat, shining sand. Every morning, before breakfast, she would come out on the beach to collect shells – delicate pink shells, sunshine-yellow fluted shells, striped grey shells, large curled shells splendid enough for a sea-king's palace. She was decorating a box for her mother to keep jewellery in.

Yesterday Mum had gone out on to the beach with her. They had walked right down to the water's edge. Mum's cheeks had been rosy, stung to colour by the wind, and she had looked quite her old self again.

"If we had lived here always," Helen had said, "instead of in dirty old London, you'd never have been ill in the first place." Still, three weeks was a good long time for a holiday, and Mum looked better every day.

From a tiny rock pool, something glittered in the sunlight. Helen stooped and picked out a dripping, fragile, almost transparent shell with delicate, scalloped edges. It glowed mysteriously as she held it to the light, and for a moment she thought she heard far-off sighing. Carefully she wiped the shell with a handkerchief, and put it in her pocket.

In the evening she told Ian about it.

"I found a rather strange, beautiful shell today," she said. "How do you suppose it came to be this flat shape, though?"

Her brother, deep in his book, did not answer.

Helen gazed through the conservatory windows, past the tiny shingle garden with its tall, white daisies and upturned boat. In the distance the sea whispered its secrets, advancing in a tumble of foam.

"I suppose the tides could have worn it down," she said, "over hundreds of years. But the tiny fronds around the edge of it and the markings – almost like eyes and a mouth. I've never seen a shell like that before."

115

Helen put the round, flat shell on the table and started to glue a tiny periwinkle on to her box.

All sides of the box were covered in shells of many different shapes and glimmering colours. She would save the special shell for the crowning glory. But she wanted the others to dry out first.

"How about a walk along the beach, Ian, before it gets dark and the tide comes in?"

At the sound of the word 'walk', Rags their terrier jumped to his feet and started to bark excitedly. He ran from the conservatory, through the dining-room and hall to the kitchen at the front of the bungalow, which overlooked a quiet road. They could hear him rattling his lead against the handle of the kitchen door.

Ian shrugged, and went on reading his book. He had changed so much in the last six months, Helen thought. He used to be enthusiastic about things once. She knew that Mum's illness had something to do with it. He brooded now, sat staring at the sea for hours, not saying a word. And whereas she loved the sea in the morning, he was fascinated by it at night.

"It says here," said Ian, turning a page, "that in some places the sea is more than six miles deep. It's freezing cold and pitch black and the fish have their own lights to swim around with."

He showed her a picture of a monstrous fish, with glaring eyes and rows of hooked teeth on the outside of its body. She shuddered a little, but said, "So that's what they put in fish-fingers now. I thought the ones Dad bought yesterday tasted funny. Come on, Ian, get your coat. Let's go for a walk."

Ian closed the book and went to get his dufflecoat from the hall.

"Who's to know what terrible creatures lurk in the depths of the sea," he whispered, "unable to rise because of the pressures. Great luminous tentacles reaching all over the floor of the ocean . . ."

Rags raced into the hall, triumphantly dragging his lead.

"There's a clever boy," said Helen. "You may not like the water, but you like a walk, don't you?"

She picked up the lead but did not fasten it to his collar, and opened the door. Rags leaped out and tore excitedly through the garden and on to the beach, crunching as he went.

The evening air had a late September chill to it and the other bungalows in the row looked desolate, locked and barred for the winter. To the west, the sun was setting in a fiery glow, outlining the tall, black chimneys of the harbour.

"Let's walk that way," said Ian, putting in his pocket the key to the back door. Dad had taken the front door key with him to the theatre. "Hope you don't mind me locking you in," he'd said, "but after the play we might go for a little celebration, if your mother feels up to it. Anyway, you can come and go by the back door until it gets dark. Don't forget about the tide, though."

They still had an hour before the water would be lapping at the poles which marked the water-line, a few yards from the bottom of the garden. Rags raced ahead, chasing after bits of driftwood. Helen chased after Rags, shouting encouragement. Ian trudged through the shingle, silent except for the sound of his plimsolls on the stones.

Soon they were beyond the neat row of bungalows and crossing the broad stretch of shingle which led to the harbour. As they walked, the brightness faded and the oil-containers edging the industrial end of the beach were upon them, huge against the darkening sky.

Helen shivered. She was glad to hear, in the distance, the voices of a family out for an evening stroll.

About to step on to a bunch of seaweed, Ian realised, just in time, that entwined in the fronds was a dead bird. Stooping down he saw the body of a seagull, feathers caked and stiff with black oil. A feeling of hatred towards the monsters which surrounded them almost overpowered him.

"Filthy, disgusting muck!" he muttered, kicking out. The massive containers gleamed a dull silver in the grey of the evening – lifeless, yet sinister.

Helen looked away towards the sea. On the dim horizon the wavering lights of a ship flashed, turned, and flashed again.

The voices of people were getting closer. Rags began to whine. The hair on his back prickled, his normally bouncy tail dropped and flattened between his legs.

Helen looked at him in surprise.

"It's only people, Rags," she started to say, but Rags was not looking in the direction of the people. He was backing away from the sea.

"What is it?" whispered Helen. Her throat had gone dry and crackly. "Ian . . . what is it?"

For the lights she had seen did not come from any ship. They formed a circle and above the lights, against the horizon, a phosphorescent, misty shape rose and fell.

Ian did not say a word. He stared, in mounting horror, at the strange apparition out at sea. Rags' whining grew in crescendo to a mournful howl.

"What on earth's got into that dog?" said a woman, climbing unskilfully over a breakwater. She wore a head-scarf, which flapped around her face. "I can't see where I'm going now. Where did that wind come from?"

Her companions followed – another woman and a middle-aged man.

"Look!" Helen cried, running towards them. "Out there . . . bobbing about in the ocean!"

"I can't see anything," said the woman. "But if it's bobbing about it'll be a buoy, I suppose, or a ship. Can you see anything, Fred?"

"There's a *boat* out there," said the man. "Over in that direction – look!"

The lights of a ship had come into view on the horizon. It seemed small beside the misty apparition. Neither the man, nor the women, could see anything else.

"Stop having us on," said the woman with the headscarf. "And do something about that dog. It's got the rabids if you ask me." They hurried on, keeping well away from Rags.

"Ian – the people on the ship!" cried Helen. "They may be in danger. What shall we do?"

"We'd better go into the town . . . get the police . . . or the coastguard or something . . ." Ian spoke slowly, with difficulty, still deeply shocked.

Helen fastened a trembling Rags to his lead, and, not daring to look back, they made their way towards a line of dingy houses which backed on to the harbour. Many of the houses were boarded up. Only one showed a light, behind torn curtains. Ian banged on the door and the curtains moved slightly, but no-one came. Across the road stood a delapidated public house. As they approached they saw 'The Captain's Rest' painted on a sign in peeling brown letters.

"Let's try there," said Helen. "At least they'll have a phone."

The saloon bar reeked of stale beer and ashtrays. The landlord, his head greased and balding, looked up suspiciously when they spoke to him, and pointed to a call-box in the lobby.

Ian dialled 999 and asked for the police.

"I'm reporting a strange . . . thing . . . in the sea, near Shoregate harbour," he said. "There's a ship out there. It may be in danger."

"And where are you ringing from?" said a briskly efficient woman's voice.

"The Captain's Rest – a pub near the harbour," said Ian. There was the briefest of pauses.

"And can I have your name and address, sir?"

He gave his name, and the address of the holiday bungalow.

"Very well, sir. We'll investigate."

He put down the telephone.

"She didn't believe me," he told Helen, "but they're going to investigate."

He sat on a faded settee and mopped his forehead.

"You know, I could do with a drink, but he'd never serve me."

"Ian, if those other people on the beach didn't see anything," said Helen, "what makes you think the police will? The crew of that ship didn't – they were moving straight towards it."

"We couldn't both have imagined it," said Ian. "And what about Rags?"

The landlord came towards them, wiping his hands on a dirty tea-towel.

"No dogs allowed in here," he said. "It's unhygienic."

Outside, the sky had darkened and the chill wind was getting stronger. Helen turned up her collar and gazed fearfully towards the sea, almost expecting a monster to rear up between the warehouses and chimneys.

"I suppose we ought to go down and see if the ship's in danger," she said. "We needn't go on to the beach. Whatever the thing is, it belongs to the sea. It couldn't climb over stones, could it?"

At first Rags dug his paws into the ground and had to be pulled by his lead back towards the beach. But gradually his resistance slackened, and once his nose caught the scent of rotting driftwood he seemed as eager as always for a romp, barking and jumping to snatch his lead from Helen's hand.

Overhead, clouds moved restlessly, edged with darkness. As they approached the moon shone full and round, transforming the surface of the water. On the horizon rocked a small, black ship. There was nothing else to be seen.

In panic, Ian ran . . .

Ian scanned the sudden, shining vista in disbelief. Then the moon disappeared and the waves lapped angrily. The tide was coming in fast.

"We'll have to hurry, Ian. We'll be cut off otherwise."

Helen still felt fear, like a leaded weight in the pit of her stomach. She longed to be back in the bungalow, with all the lights turned on, and with music blaring loudly.

"We can go by road most of the way," said Ian, "but we'll have to do the last bit along the coast. Come on, hurry."

The seafront bungalows were linked by carports. There

was no way of getting from the front to the back of them. They approached the first bungalow in the row and climbed down to the beach. Great waves surged over and above the waterline.

"Which is it?" yelled Ian, tugging at a terrified Rags. Each garden looked the same in the darkness, each bungalow stood blank and empty.

. . . but Helen whispered, "Who are you?"

"That one – with the boat."

Soaked and shivering, they stumbled up the pathway and into the conservatory. The moon disappeared behind clouds again. Ian went through to the dining-room, switched on the light, and for the first time that evening looked at his watch.

"It's time for the news," he said. "I'll turn the radio on. Surely someone else must have seen something."

The announcer was concerned with the state of the economy and progressed from that to the state of the weather and football. Rags shook himself miserably and crouched before the electric fire, trying to will it to life and staring reproachfully at Helen. But Helen, pressed up against the window of the dark conservatory, did not even notice. She was aware only of the nagging, sick feeling at the pit of her stomach. The conservatory had glass doors and windows, giving a panoramic view of the sea. And as Helen stared, a misty luminous glow came from the water, although no moon was shining.

Rags whimpered, and crawled under the table.

"Ian," she whispered, full of dread. "It's come again . . . Look."

The creature seemed to have no movement of its own. It was pushed forwards with the waves, backwards, then forwards again, nearer and nearer to the edge of the water, looming larger with each progression. The silvery blue glow was intensifying. Ian could see now the huge, jelly-like substance, the mass of tentacles like undulating, transparent snakes. He realised with horror that the light around the creature's body – if it could be called a body – were great staring eyes.

In cold panic he rushed to the front of the house, away from the terrible vision. The only possible way of escape was through the kitchen window. He climbed up on to the draining-board, slipping on the wet, polished steel.

Helen continued to gaze, trance-like, through the conservatory window. Slowly, the ice in her stomach was beginning to thaw. A realisation was coming to her of a strange, dark world . . . a huge creature powerfully working itself against the pressures which each moment threatened to crush it into oblivion, driven by an instinct stronger than its own survival, rising slowly upwards, yearning . . . searching . . .

"What are you?" she whispered, mesmerised by the relentless movement, the unearthly pallor. "What do you want from us?"

Then she was suddenly aware of something else glowing, in the darkness of the room. It was the shell. It shone from the table beside her, faintly at first, then with a strange blue light. The apparition, as if in response, flooded the sky and sea with radiance.

Helen, still in a trance, rose and took the small, flat, shining disc from the table. It pulsed with warm, strong vibrations, the tiny fronds a-quiver with life.

"Why," she whispered, in wonder, "you're not a shell at all."

She opened the door of the conservatory and walked slowly, deliberately, down the path. The monster loomed over her, tall as a ship, filling the night.

She held out her hand. The tiny creature in her palm shone so brightly that sparks seemed to spill, but it did not burn her. Gently she placed it on the shore and stood, unafraid, listening to the sighing of the sea as the mother reclaimed her own.

The huge creature was moving away now. Helen watched as it faded, slowly dissolving into the night air, now an outline, now no more than a mist, blown by sea-breezes. Soon only the great lighted eyes remained, undulating with the waves. She saw them grow smaller and smaller until they were no more than specks of light, like tiny stars in an immense, watery universe.

Then she turned, and walked back to the bungalow.

SOMETHING QUEER ON THE MOOR

by ROGER MALISSON

Granny Appleyard plonked her stick down firmly on the kitchen floor and declared, "I'm not goin' back."

"But, Mum, we haven't much room for you here," said Mrs. Appleyard worriedly.

Ronnie, who had just arrived home from school, looked from his mother to his granny and sighed. "If I went back with you, Gran . . . ?" he suggested hopefully.

The old lady shook her head, a look of sharp determination in her faded blue eyes. "I'm not goin' to stay up there tonight. It's dangerous, I tell you. There's summat queer on the Moor."

"But what?" Ronnie's mother asked anxiously. "If it's a prowler, well, we can call the police – "

"Police is no good," said Granny Appleyard contemptuously. "Ain't no prowler. Too big for a prowler," she added as a cryptic afterthought.

Ronnie and his mother exchanged hopeless glances, and

Ronnie shrugged. What could you do with a stubborn old woman who had a fixed idea in her head, when you had no means of removing it? Or her, come to that. Ronnie was fond of his granny but he groaned mentally at the thought of the hard sofa he would be trying to sleep on that night if Granny Appleyard insisted on staying. She would have to take his bed, because there wasn't a spare one for guests.

"Sure you're not imagining things, Gran?" he asked casually.

Granny Appleyard leaped to her feet, hopping mad. "You saying I'm goin' senile, young Ronnie? 'Cause you're not too big to be spanked for your cheek!"

But Ronnie was. In fact, the top of her neat grey head was just level with his shoulder. Ronnie smiled apologetically, and Granny Appleyard sat down again, disgruntled.

"But you've never actually seen anything, have you?" Ronnie's mother persisted. "I mean, you said yourself it's only a feeling you have that somebody's out there."

"It's true enough," snapped the old lady. "And I'm not goin' crazy. I tell you, there's – "

"We know," sighed Ronnie. "There's something queer on the Moor."

Heatherton Moor was a bleak area of land stretching from the outskirts of Heatherton, the village where Ronnie lived, to the cultivated fields of the farms beyond. Granny Appleyard's cottage stood isolated on a moorland hill, some four miles from Heatherton. She had lived there all her life, alone since Ronnie's grandfather had died and left her a widow. She was kind, a little irritable as elderly people often are, but sensible enough usually.

Leaving his mother and Gran to their argument in the kitchen, Ronnie wandered up to his bedroom to unpack his satchel. It wasn't often, he had to admit, that Granny Appleyard took strange ideas into her head, though there had been that time when she'd insisted that the new vicar was a Communist spy, and refused to come to church while he was there. Come to think of it, the new vicar *had* left without a word to anyone, and in rather a hurry . . .

But that had nothing to do with the present case. Something queer on the Moor, indeed! There was nothing at all to populate Heatherton Moor except for a few rabbits and an old woman's imagination. There wasn't much homework tonight. He could probably finish it by dinner time if he started right away.

When Ronnie's father came home from the steel works he took the whole business as a huge joke, but said that his mother must stay with them if she felt nervous about returning to her cottage.

"Then there's the cat," mumbled Granny Appleyard over dinner.

"What cat?" asked Ronnie's father.

"My Tiddles," explained Granny grumpily. "Up there she is, locked out, likely hungry, an' summat queer rambling about on the Moor."

"Oh, she'll manage for one night, Mum," said Ronnie's mother reassuringly. "We can pick her up tomorrow."

The old woman poked her food about moodily with her fork. "Gets cold up there, these nights," she remarked.

Ronnie grinned at his father, who raised his eyes to heaven. There would be no peace until the cat was safe.

"You've got a Union meeting tonight, haven't you, Dad? I'll fetch Tiddles, Gran."

Her face lit up.

"Would you, Ronnie? There's a good lad. Nothing to fear in daylight, there isn't, and you can be back before dark if you hurry."

"Right, Gran." By now, Ronnie was resigned to sleeping on the sofa.

Bees hummed and played about the wild moorland flowers, and distant birdsong sounded on the sunny air. The long, fresh summer evening was ideal for a walk across the moors. Unless, of course, you had just passed up a game of football for a rather silly errand.

Ronnie tramped on over the heathery downs. He took the shortest route he knew to the cottage, but he lost more time and daylight than he realised in dawdling and thinking. He wasn't usually a day-dreamer, but his imagination began to play on Granny Appleyard's mysterious half-tale.

I hope I can find the wretched cat when I get there, he thought. What if there really is something prowling the Moor? Frankenstein's monster, perhaps, or some nameless shapeless Thing from the Bog. He grinned to himself. Well for one thing, you didn't meet a vast number of mad German scientists in the little streets of Heatherton, and for another they didn't have any bogs for Things to crawl out of.

All right then, said his imagination, what about a man-eating fish with a million tearing teeth? Or a deformed humanoid alien from a planet in space? There again it would be extremely difficult, not to say impossible, for a fish, savage or otherwise, to exist on Heatherton Moor, what with the nearest pond a good six miles away. Ronnie stopped short and scanned the horizon. Not a spaceship in sight, worse luck. Nothing exciting ever happened to him.

He trudged up the last steep mile to Granny Appleyard's little white-washed cottage. Tiddles, true to form, was sitting on the doormat. Idly licking a paw, the cat watched him approach; she was the only living creature he had seen on the way.

"Hello, Tiddles." Ronnie opened the cottage door with his key and the cat wound herself against his legs, purring. Food was surely on the way.

Inside the cottage everything was as neat as always. Ronnie set a saucer of milk for the cat and went upstairs to collect some clothes for his Granny. It might be a long visit.

As he was pushing a dressing-gown into the case he had brought, Ronnie slowly became aware of an unfamiliar noise. It was a whispering, rustling sound. He dropped the case and hurried to the window. There was nothing to be seen near the cottage, nor on the rolling moorlands beyond. Listening hard in the silence that fell, he tried to think what might have made the sound. Perhaps a breeze in the chimney, though he fancied it was more like the noise of something huge, trying to move stealthily . . .

But that was foolish. All the same, he quickly finished packing the case, snapped it shut and ran downstairs, where he was relieved to see Tiddles crouched over her dish, still lapping placidly. An animal would have sensed anything strange, and taken fright.

He took a last glance round; all was in order. It was getting dusk, time to set off for home. Ronnie took his case in one hand and made to lift Tiddles with the other.

Suddenly the noise came again. This time it was a dry crackling sound, as if someone had fallen into the heap of firewood Granny kept in the yard.

Without pausing to think Ronnie made straight for the back door, unbolted it and stepped outside. There was nobody in the yard. Ronnie took a deep breath, and realised that he was shaking slightly. No wonder Granny had been so scared with all the odd noises around her home. It couldn't be the wind, the evening was too still, so perhaps –

There was a shrill yeowl and Tiddles sprang out of the door after him. She stood rigid and bristling for a moment, giving an excellent imitation of an animated hairbrush, then streaked out of the yard and over the Moor for Heatherton as if the devil were after her.

No sooner had she gone than the back door slammed with a terrible crash that made Ronnie jump violently. Badly scared now, he stared nervously at the cottage. Something was inside! As he watched, a great shadow fell across the kitchen window, and the door rattled as though it were being opened by hands not used to opening doors . . .

Ronnie did not stay to see any more. He turned and fled, taking the road that wound about the back of the hill to Heatherton. But as he ran, he heard above the rasping of his breath and the thudding of his heart the steady impact on the ground of mighty feet behind him. He was being followed! All he knew about the thing was that it was enormous, bigger than anything he had ever seen, and for some awful unknown reason it was chasing him down the hill!

He ran like the wind through the gathering dusk, not daring to look behind for fear of slackening speed, and all the while the effortlessly regular beat of the giant footsteps pursued him down the narrow moorland path. Leaping over puddles and swerving round rocks that littered the track, a terrified Ronnie ran for his life. The creature padded close behind with untiring energy, and he knew his only hope was to outdistance it. Whatever happened it mustn't catch up!

Then, as he sprinted round a bend in the road, the distant lights of Heatherton twinkled into view. Ahead loomed the familiar flat milestone with *'Heatherton – Two Miles'* inscribed upon it. But could he keep up his furious race to reach safety?

Just as he felt he could run no more, the terror behind him lessened. The great pounding footsteps grew fainter, and Ronnie sensed that the creature was losing ground. The presence behind him was fading – he had managed to outrun it! Perhaps it could not leave the Moor. Ronnie risked a glance behind him; there was nothing to be seen.

Panting, he slowed to a trot. The lights of Heatherton winked at him, comfortingly near. Ronnie reached the milestone and stopped, straining his eyes and ears into the rapidly-fading darkness. There was no trace of anything weird.

He collapsed exhausted on to the stone, thankful that the danger was past, half-ready to believe that the crazy moorland chase had been the product of his imagination, like a nightmare. He sank his head and raised his shoulders, the athlete's way of getting air quickly into the lungs, and stretched his weary legs. Another few minutes, he thought, and he would be safe and warm at home.

Suddenly, Ronnie glanced down at the ground. Beside the milestone was a foot, a huge hairy foot joined to a shaggy brownish leg! Ronnie's head was about level with the top of the ankle. Numbly he stared at the foot, too shocked and amazed to raise his eyes any higher.

A great voice sounded from several yards above him.

"That was a good race," it rumbled. "Shall we have another one like that?"